"R.J. Patterson does a fantast
interested. I look forward to more from this talented author."

- Aaron Patterson
bestselling author of SWEET DREAMS

DEAD SHOT

"Small town life in southern Idaho might seem quaint and idyllic to
some. But when local newspaper reporter Cal Murphy begins to uncover a series of strange deaths that are linked to a sticky spider web
of deception, the lid on the peaceful town is blown wide open.
Told with all the energy and bravado of an old pro, first-timer
R.J. Patterson hits one out of the park his first time at bat with *Dead
Shot*. It's that good."

- Vincent Zandri
bestselling author of THE REMAINS

"You can tell R.J. knows what it's like to live in the newspaper
world, but with *Dead Shot*, he's proven that he also can write one
heck of a murder mystery."

- Josh Katzowitz
NFL writer for CBSSports.com
& author of Sid Gillman: Father of the Passing Game

"Patterson has a mean streak about a mile wide and puts his two
main characters through quite a horrible ride, which makes for good
reading."

- Richard D., reader

DEAD LINE

"This book kept me on the edge of my seat the whole time. I didn't
really want to put it down. R.J. Patterson has hooked me. I'll be
back for more."

- Bob Behler
3-time Idaho broadcaster of the year
and play-by-play voice for Boise State football

"Like a John Grisham novel, from the very start I was pulled right into the story and couldn't put the book down. It was as if I personally knew and cared about what happened to each of the main characters. Every chapter ended with so much excitement and suspense I had to continue to read until I learned how it ended, even though it kept me up until 3:00 A.M.

- Ray F., reader

DEAD IN THE WATER

"In Dead in the Water, R.J. Patterson accurately captures the action-packed saga of a what could be a real-life college football scandal. The sordid details will leave readers flipping through the pages as fast as a hurry-up offense."

- Mark Schlabach,
ESPN college sports columnist and
co-author of *Called to Coach*
and *Heisman: The Man Behind the Trophy*

THE WARREN OMISSIONS

"What can be more fascinating than a super high concept novel that reopens the conspiracy behind the JFK assassination while the threat of a global world war rests in the balance? With his new novel, *The Warren Omissions*, former journalist turned bestselling author R.J. Patterson proves he just might be the next worthy successor to Vince Flynn."

- Vincent Zandri
bestselling author of THE REMAINS

OTHER TITLES BY
R.J. PATTERSON

ANY MEANS NECESSARY

A Brady Hawk novel

R.J. PATTERSON

ANY MEANS NECESSARY
© Copyright 2018 R.J. Patterson

First Print Edition 2019

Cover Design by Books Covered

Published in the United States of America
Green E-Books
Boise Idaho 83713

*For Chad, a great soldier
and a great American*

CHAPTER 1

**Arabian Sea,
off the coast of Somalia**

BRADY HAWK TUGGED on the rope tied to his harness as he sat suspended off the side of the ocean freighter and out of sight. Satisfied that the cable keeping him tethered to the grappling hook above was taut, he took a deep breath and closed his eyes. He filtered out the sounds of the water lapping against the hull and the seagulls circling overhead. All he wanted to hear was the conversation occurring on the deck.

"How much longer?" a man asked in Arabic.

"Fifteen minutes and everything will be secured."

"Excellent."

Hawk couldn't see anyone from his vantage point, but he didn't have to. For starters, he recognized the voice of Asad Kudrati the moment he started speaking. The Somali pirate was all business, but his voice had been frequently recorded on surveillance footage between him and other illegal arms dealers. Yet this was the first time Hawk had been in such close proximity to the man.

But Hawk didn't need to see everything. His real eyes on the operation belonged to Alex, his wife and partner on all endeavors commissioned by the Phoenix Foundation. Comfortably tracking all the action a few miles away from a U.S. Navy destroyer, she relayed pertinent information to Hawk, following the entire operation from a satellite feed.

Hawk strained to listen as the conversation on deck fell silent.

"They're almost finished loading their three boats," Alex said. "Kudrati is on the port side now. And he's drinking straight from a bottle of some sort."

"Roger that," Hawk whispered. "Let me know when it's time to move."

"Will do."

Hawk closed his eyes and took momentary pleasure in the sea breeze. The smell of the salty water always brought back plenty of memories, some of spending time on the beaches of Northern California as a kid visiting his grandmother, some while training with the Navy SEALs in Southern California. The two experiences couldn't have been more polar opposites when it came to enjoyment.

Opening his eyes, he smiled and shook his head

at the thought of his current situation. He was amused at the twisted path he found himself on after uncovering the list of people affiliated with the Russian arms dealer Andrei Orlovsky.

You never know what adventures snorkeling in Venice will lead to.

Hawk pulled out his binoculars. The sun flickered faintly off some reflective object on the deck of *U.S.S. The Sullivans.* The ship was still there, ready to make a move when necessary.

"He's coming your way," Alex said. "Get ready because the deck is clear."

Hawk maneuvered into position, grasping the rope with both hands while stabilizing himself with his feet.

"On your command," Hawk said.

"Swing to your left in 3,2, 1," Alex said. "Now!"

Hawk swung to one side and then the other before grabbing onto the railing and flinging himself over. Kudrati had his back turned to Hawk when he stealthily landed. Untethering from the rope and drawing his weapon, Hawk rushed toward Kudrati. Hawk kept his index finger over his lips and eyed Kudrati closely. With a slight nod to acknowledge the command, Kudrati followed Hawk's lead as they descended below deck and into the captain's quarters. Vacated after the pirates boarded the ship, the room was devoid of any people but had been tossed by pirates looking for a little extra something for their pockets.

"In here," Hawk said, using his gun to direct Kudrati inside.

Kudrati shuffled over to a table and a pair of chairs.

"Sit down," Hawk said, speaking in Arabic. He proceeded to lock the door before walking over to his prisoner.

Kudrati eased into one of the seats and kept his left hand up in a posture of surrender while the right one clung to a bottle of baijiu. Hawk motioned for Kudrati to slide the liquor across the table, a gesture that was followed.

Hawk grabbed the drink and smelled the rim. He shook his head, screwing his face up.

"How do you drink this stuff?" Hawk asked in English.

"It's an acquired taste," Kudrati responded. "After you rob enough Chinese freighters, you just get used to it. The bastards don't drink anything else."

Hawk returned the bottle to the table and settled into the chair across from his prisoner.

"I suppose you didn't bring me down here to discuss the distinct ingredients of Chinese liquor, did you?" Kudrati asked.

A faint smile flickered across Hawk's lips. "I already know how it burns—and also how unsatisfying it is."

"Yet it's the most popular liquor in the world."

"Only because they haven't figured out how to make whiskey with cheaper ingredients."

Kudrati chuckled. "One would assume."

Hawk brandished his gun, training it on Kudrati. "Well, I'm not assuming anything when it comes to how you found out about the cargo on this particular ship. I want you to tell me for yourself."

"I don't know what you're talking about. I'm a pirate. I steal things."

Hawk leaned forward. "This is different. I know what this vessel was carrying—and so did you. I also know that you're connected to a certain Russian arms dealer."

Kudrati laughed. "If you know so much, why are we even having this conversation?"

"Because I need to hear it directly from you to confirm. And then I have some other questions for you."

"You won't hear anything from me. But I will hear your screams as you die when my men swarm upon you."

Hawk narrowed his eyes. "Your men will be more interested in saving themselves in a few minutes.

They'll forget you were ever their captain."

"You underestimate my men."

Hawk leaned back in his seat before responding. "Are you still there, Alex?"

"Just waiting for your word," she said.

"Let the commander know that it's time."

Kudrati shook his head. "Do you think your little game is going to scare me?"

Hawk stood and backed toward the window, tapping on it with his gun. "Why don't you take a look?"

Kudrati slowly rose to his feet and strode over toward the window. He peered through it before looking at Hawk. "It appears you have brought reinforcements," Kudrati said. "That doesn't change my position. My men are going to remain until I'm aboard with them."

"Then your men are fools and will soon be dead. Now, perhaps we should start over. Where did you learn about this particular shipment?"

"I already told you, I—"

"This time I want the truth. Did Andrei Orlovsky tell you about what was on board?"

"Andrei who?"

Hawk slammed his fist onto the table. "Don't play dumb with me. You know exactly who I'm talking about."

"I'm afraid I don't. I'm truly sorry that you have wasted your time."

"Tell me what you know about Obsidian."

Kudrati shook his head again. "What is an Obsidian?"

"Your feigned ignorance won't get you very far with me. I happen to have proof that you're tied to the group. And if you want to live, you will tell me what you know about them."

"Your arrogance will be your downfall," Kudrati said before breaking into a hearty laugh. "You Americans never cease to amaze me with your brazen bravado."

Before Hawk could respond, thundering footsteps pounded down the hall. He raced around the table and placed his hand over Kudrati's mouth and a gun to his head. "If you know what's good for you, you won't say a word."

Kudrati ripped Hawk's hand away and screamed in Arabic. "I'm in here."

Hawk pistol-whipped Kudrati in the head, knocking him out.

"Alex, what's your ETA?" Hawk asked.

"We'll be in range in five minutes," she said. "But I have a drone that will be in position in a matter of seconds."

"Take one of their boats out," Hawk said. "They need something to retreat to."

"Roger that."

The pounding on the door outside grew louder as the men called for Kudrati. They shouted their demands that he be released. When Hawk didn't respond, they resorted to threats.

As the rancorous mob continued outside, Hawk couldn't resist the urge to answer.

"Save yourselves and return to your ship," he said in Arabic.

The men outside laughed before resuming their pounding on the door.

"Give us Kudrati," they started to chant in unison.

The sound of a missile annihilating one of the boats on the port side ended the men's mantra. Instead of shouting, Hawk heard only their footfalls growing fainter as they raced up the steps to the ship's deck. With the captain's quarters on the starboard side, Hawk couldn't see what had happened with the drone strike, but he didn't need to. The anguish emanating from the men above told Hawk all he needed to know.

Kudrati moaned as he started to regain consciousness.

"Your men are gone," Hawk said. "They scrambled away, terrified of the drone circling their ships outside."

"You bastard," Kudrati said. "Do you know what you've done?"

Hawk nodded. "Exactly what I set out to do."

"Those men are innocent. They know nothing."

"They're far from innocent. And they know exactly what they're doing. As a result, they're going to pay a steep price. But if you want to blame someone, blame yourself. If you had just told me what I wanted to know, perhaps they all could've been shepherded to safety."

"Please," Kudrati pleaded, "they don't know anything. They are just men I hired to help with this job."

"Men you hired to plunder and steal from a specific Chinese boat. Now, tell me again about your relationship with Andrei Orlovsky."

"Since you seem to know so much about it, why don't you tell me?"

"I'm not here to play games. I need answers, and I need them now."

"It's too late for that," Kudrati said. "I'm as good as dead after what you've done."

"There were military weapons on this ship, the kind of weapons that aren't available except on the black market. And you knew all about them. Who were you going to sell them to? Was this to arm another terrorist plot against the U.S.?"

"You self-important Americans," Kudrati said, shaking his head. "You never cease to amaze me in your view of the world. You think you are at the center of everything. Well, I have news for you— you're not. And this war that's coming isn't one that will be waged against you. It's one that will be waged against everyone everywhere. These allegiances will not be defined by borders."

"And yet you seem to have no problem helping these tyrants."

Kudrati groaned. "Not you, me, or a thousand nations could stop what these men are doing. There comes a time in a man's life where he must decide between idealism and self-preservation. And in this situation, there's only one choice that will keep me alive—and that's what I prefer."

"I haven't found those two things to be mutually exclusive."

"By the time you realize that they are, it will be too late."

Hawk grabbed Kudrati by his collar and led him out of the room.

"If you don't want to talk with me now, I will have to persuade you in other ways."

"Don't waste your time," Kudrati said. "You'll never get a word out of me."

"If you don't talk, you're no good to me."

"What are you going to do then? Kill me?"

Hawk stopped and eyed Kudrati. "You might

need to rethink that theory on self-preservation."

They resumed their trek through the narrow corridor before ascending to the upper deck. The drone circling overhead provided plenty of incentive for the pirates to speed away from the Chinese freighter with all its weapons. Hawk looked off the port side and saw the *U.S.S. The Sullivans* churning toward them.

"Alex?" Hawk asked.

"I'm listening."

"Can you take care of those ships for me? We can't have those weapons falling into the wrong hands."

"Roger that. We can't have those weapons falling into anyone's hands."

Moments later, two missile strikes from the drone put a fiery end to the pirates' boats. Hawk waited to see if anyone survived. If they did, he couldn't see them through the two plumes of smoke rising off the water.

"I hope you're proud of yourself," Kudrati said. "Those men had families. They were just trying to survive."

Hawk shook his head. "And those men would've sold dangerous weapons to killers who would've used them to murder other men with families. I live in the gray areas of this world, Mr. Kudrati, and it's a big place."

Before Kudrati could respond, a bullet exploded in his chest. He crumpled to the ground, screaming in agony.

Hawk knelt next to his captive and put his hand on the bleeding wound.

"It's no use," Kudrati said. "I told you I was good as dead."

A few seconds later, Kudrati exhaled his final breath.

Hawk wanted to stand up and see where the shot came from. There was no other ship around except the *U.S.S. The Sullivans.*

"What just happened?" Alex squawked on the coms.

"Kudrati's dead from a sniper shot," Hawk replied.

"That's what it looked like, but—how? Who could've made that shot? And where did it come from?"

"I'd love to investigate further," Hawk said, "However, I'm not too keen on the idea of standing up and searching for the shooter. My first inclination is to assume that it had to come from the deck of your ship."

"You think Obsidian has a soldier in its pocket who's on board?"

"It'd be foolish not to at least consider that possibility. Obsidian seems to have people everywhere else. Why not the U.S. Navy?"

"It's hard to argue against that."

Hawk sighed. "None of that changes the fact that we just lost our first good lead on someone with connections to Obsidian. Someone has been reading our mail."

CHAPTER 2

Washington, D.C.

HAWK AND ALEX ENTERED the Phoenix Foundation offices and trudged upstairs to meet with J.D. Blunt. The former Texas senator overseeing the special program working in conjunction with the CIA sat in his office with his feet propped up on the edge of his desk. With a cigar dangling from his mouth, he waved them inside once they made eye contact.

"Glad you two made it back alive," Blunt said.

"There should've been three of us," Hawk said as he settled into his seat.

Alex eased into her chair and nodded in agreement.

"We still don't know where that shot came from," she said. "I looked at all the surveillance footage from the deck and couldn't find anything suspicious, much less someone firing a long range shot from *The Sullivans* in the direction of that Chinese freighter. It's baffling."

"Well, there's nothing we can do about it now, but there is something else you need to look into for me," Blunt said. "And this kind of problem can have far-reaching consequences if we don't act right away."

Hawk shifted in his seat. "What kind of problem are we talking about here?"

"The kind that has to do with a cyber attack," Blunt said.

Alex's eyes lit up. "Did you say cyber attacks?"

Blunt smiled and leaned forward in his chair.

"I thought this might excite you, Alex," he said. "Your expertise is going to come in extremely handy as we try to sort this problem out."

"We've received several reports over the past few days about blackmail attempts occurring against U.S. Senators, starting with Louisiana's Bernard Fontenot," Blunt said.

"Fontenot," Hawk said as he closed his eyes. "I remember something about him. Wasn't he involved in a campaign finance scandal about eight years ago? He got caught taking a large sum money from a foreign national who was never named. Fontenot claimed it was an oversight. But for the sake of this investigation, let's not worry about that."

"Why?" Alex asked. "That could be quite a significant revelation if it turns out the senator is getting outside pressure from someone who isn't a citizen."

"It would surely open up a can of worms that I don't think anyone on Capitol Hill or the White House wants at this point," Blunt said. "Just keep the scope of this investigation narrow. We need to know who's behind these attacks, specifically Fontenot's. If we're able to correctly identify the person or group orchestrating these efforts, that will go a long way in helping us figure out how to stop them."

"Pulling the plug is always the easiest solution, if you ask me," Hawk said.

"That's the easy *part*," Alex said. "The hard part is finding the right plug to tug on."

"And at the moment, we're somewhat in the dark about what the end game of this organization is," Blunt said. "And that's why you need to start with Fontenot. The group has made specific demands of him."

"Such as . . . ?" Alex said.

"Fontenot, who is up for reelection next year, is head of the Senate's prestigious intelligence committee. This group wants him to step down. And in exchange for his cooperation, they've promised not to release a handful of private communiqués they allegedly received from some anonymous source. We all know that's a big steaming pile of bullshit. Whoever these people are, they hacked into the computer system on Capitol Hill and found dirt on a handful people."

"Who's to say they're going to stop any time soon?" Alex asked.

"Exactly, which is why they need to be stopped sooner rather than later," Blunt said. "Before long, all of Washington will be nothing but puppets in the hands of this clandestine group."

"Could it be Obsidian?" Hawk asked.

Blunt shrugged. "Maybe, maybe not. We still don't have enough information. And that's why I need you two focused and fully engaged in solving this mystery."

"We'll follow the evidence, sir, though there seems to be so little of it at the moment."

"Actually, we know a few things more than what I just told you," Blunt said. "To begin with, we know the attacks are originating in North Korea."

"And you aren't suspecting the North Koreans?" Hawk asked before his mouth fell agape.

"Everyone is a suspect at this point," Blunt said. "The North Koreans, the Chinese, the Russians—hell, we've even batted around the possibility that this might be the work of some drug lord in Mexico. The bottom line is that we just don't know who is most likely behind this. And that's what I want you to find out."

Hawk nodded. "I see. So, what about the CIA?"

"What about them?" Blunt asked.

"Why aren't they getting involved in this?"

"This situation happens to be too intertwined in politics," Blunt said, shaking his head. "They don't want to be used in any partisan attacks from either side of the aisle. If we can handle this discreetly before news about the leaks slips out to the press, they'll avoid a dicey public relations nightmare—and we'll know the identity as well as the true intent of the group taking this type of action."

Hawk smiled. "Do you enjoy just waving your magic wand from your ivory tower here to make problems go away?"

Blunt chuckled and nodded. "Probably almost as much as you enjoy being the one to make the problems disappear."

"Does Fontenot know what we do?" Alex asked.

"As a member of the Senate Intelligence Committee, he's aware that there's a secret task force employed by the CIA to handle situations like this," Blunt said. "However, he doesn't know all the inner workings or who's even involved."

"So, if we pay him a visit, will he be able to trace us back to the Phoenix Foundation?" Alex asked.

Blunt held up his index finger and fished around in his top desk drawer. After a few seconds, he held up a pair of identification badges.

"I've been meaning to give these to you for a

while," Blunt said, sliding them across his desk toward Hawk and Alex. "This will enable you to access most government buildings here and speak directly with higher level personnel. And if anyone searches for you, you'll show up in the CIA's database under these new aliases."

"Special Agent Roman and Special Agent Miller," Alex said, reading off the tags.

"No first names?" Hawk asked.

"None needed," Blunt said. "It keeps everything more streamlined. If someone asks for a check on you, the CIA will find you in the system and be able to verify your employment."

"Sounds simple enough," Hawk said.

A knock on Blunt's door interrupted their conversation. It was Linda, Blunt's secretary.

"What is it, Linda?" Blunt asked.

"I'm sorry to bother you, sir, but you told me to notify you if something happened to a member of congress."

"And?" Blunt asked, waiting for the rest of the message.

"It's Senator Mike Paxton, sir. He's resigning effective immediately. During his impromptu press conference, he didn't come straight out and say why, but social media is exploding with stories about him having an affair. According to some of my sources, he's paying the woman off."

Blunt chuckled. "If by sources you mean some random people on Twitter, we can hold off on positing any theories for the time being."

She nodded and then disappeared down the hall.

"What committee is he on?" Alex asked.

"The Senate Commerce Committee," Blunt said.

"The Commerce Committee and Intelligence Committee? Those are vastly different ends of the spectrum," Hawk said. "If this is some orchestrated attack, the end game is still quite murky."

Blunt nodded in agreement before his phone rang again.

"If you'll excuse me for just one more moment," Blunt said. "I need to take this call."

Hawk looked at Alex and knit his brow. The connection between Fontenot and Paxton seemed weak, maybe even mere coincidence. But Hawk wasn't about to come to that conclusion, especially not without an exhaustive investigation into it.

"I see," Blunt said. "I appreciate you letting me know. I'll be in touch soon."

Blunt hung up and sighed. He rubbed his face and grimaced.

"What was that about?" Hawk asked. "More bad news?"

Blunt nodded. "That was a call from one of my

contacts over at Langley. Apparently, just within the last two hours, there are seven other targeted senators who've reported that they've been pressured to step down or else embarrassing information would be released."

"This is bigger than we thought," Hawk said.

Blunt dismissed them with the back of his hand.

"Hurry up and get going," Blunt said. "Senator Fontenot is expecting you to drop by and visit him at his home."

He tapped a folder on his desk. Hawk picked up the documents and started scanning them.

"That has everything you need to know on Fontenot—and a whole lot more," Blunt said. "Read it along the way. We don't have any time to waste."

Hawk flipped through the document, but was snapped back to reality by Alex tugging on his shirtsleeve.

"We need to get going, Hawk," she said. "I'll read everything to you along the way."

CHAPTER 3

SENATOR BERNARD FONTENOT swilled the cognac around in his glass and stared out at the choppy water of the Potomac River. The steady breeze blowing across the water tousled Fontenot's hair. He finger combed it back into place for a moment before suffering another attack.

The hell with it.

He took another swig of his drink and paced around his back porch, waiting for his guests to arrive. He preferred to conduct all of his meetings within the comfortable confines of his senate office at the Capitol Building, but not when the nature of his business was so sensitive. While he had never heard of Special Agents Roman and Miller before today, he did a little sleuthing and learned that the Miller agent was a woman—and a rather attractive one at that.

Fontenot had just endured a nasty divorce, likely due to the fact that he'd spent more time in Washington than in Baton Rouge since getting elected.

That was ten years ago, plenty of time to drift apart from Jennifer. After he learned about her affair, he considered how to best handle the situation for the kids. If he lost his senate seat because he didn't have his wife standing by him, so be it. His divorce wasn't his doing—and it proved that he was committed to serving his constituents, even at great cost to his personal life. But that was two years ago, and the next election was fast approaching. And Special Agent Miller was definitely someone he could see himself pursuing. A strong woman with Washington connections was a perfect marriage candidate for him. It was something he could only think about if the two agents could make his other more pressing problem disappear.

However, Fontenot's foray into dreamland was abruptly nixed when he saw the diamond on her finger as she walked onto the porch with Special Agent Roman.

Fontenot forced a smile in an attempt to be cordial and hide his disappointment.

"Good afternoon," he said, offering his hand. "I've been expecting you two."

The two agents shook his hand and introduced themselves.

"Would you two like something to drink?" Fontenot asked, hoisting his glass into the air.

"Hennessy Timeless. I bought five bottles from the limited release, and it's still the best cognac you'll ever put to your lips."

"No, thank you," Agent Roman said.

"And you?" Fontenot said, turning to Agent Miller.

"I'm not much for cognac, but thank you for the generous offer."

"Very well then," Fontenot said before gesturing toward the two couches near the corner of the porch. "Why don't we have a seat and discuss this predicament I've been put in."

The two agents sat as Fontenot suggested. He set down his drink and then eased into the couch across from his guests.

"So, how much do you two know about my situation?" he asked.

"Enough to know that you're being co-opted by someone who has access to all your information," Agent Miller said.

Fontenot was distracted by her smile, even though he realized she was already spoken for. He sighed and then gazed out toward the water.

"That's putting it lightly," Fontenot said. "I heard that you two are the best team in all of Washington to make a problem like this go away."

Agent Roman chuckled. "We have a PR team that likes to oversell our services."

"If you can eliminate this problem for me, I don't care if your track record is inflated or not. This kind of international meddling in U.S. politics is what everyone has been afraid of. None of this should even be an issue, but this is the current political climate we live in. Not much we can do about that."

"Well, let's see if we can address the issue of someone blackmailing you," Agent Miller said. "Why don't you start from the top and tell us what this is all about?"

Fontenot picked up his glass and took a long pull on it before setting it back down. He leaned forward on the couch and licked his lips.

"When I was growing up, my father was a diplomat," Fontenot explained. "We lived all over the world from the time I was ten until I graduated from high school and enrolled at Harvard. When I was getting ready to go into the ninth grade, my father was transferred to the embassy in India. My parents weren't satisfied with any of the English-speaking schools there, so they opted to send me to the La Gruyère Institute, a boarding school in Switzerland. It was a place for the children of elite parents, though I'm still not sure how my father justified the cost to send me there. But he did. And it was there that I met Yuri Azarov."

Agent Miller's eyes widened. "Yuri Azarov? *The* Yuri Azarov?"

Fontenot nodded. "Yes, Yuri Azarov, the Russian Secretary of State. We were just kids at the time, having fun and going to school. He was just Yuri to me—and still is."

"Wait," Agent Roman said, throwing his hands up in the air. "You're *still* friends with Azarov?"

Fontenot nodded. "Going against all the advice that I've received over the years, we are still friends. I know it might seem strange to you, but sometimes there are bonds forged that go beyond our patriotic leanings."

"You are aware that he's turned a blind eye to atrocities committed on the Crimean peninsula," Agent Roman said. "He could put an end to so many questionable Russian government practices if he had any common decency."

Fontenot shook his head and looked down before responding. He glanced up at the two agents and took a deep breath. "Everything isn't always as it seems, Agent Roman. Reality is always far more complicated than issuing a simple edict to make a country's sins vanish. Absolution often requires a significant purge. And that's definitely not something Yuri can accomplish on his own. While he can influence some policies, I can assure you his presence in the office of Secretary of State has yielded far more positive results than you will likely ever know about."

"And who told you about this?" Agent Roman asked. "Was this something he told you about himself?"

"I have no reason to hold him suspect," Fontenot said. "Yuri has been a longtime confidant to me. I've never caught him lying to me nor have I ever known him to be deceitful."

"People can change, Senator," Agent Miller said.

"I know because I certainly have—and for the better, just like Yuri."

"Don't be so naïve," Agent Roman said. "If you're only hearing the story from him, you're likely not hearing everything."

"Your predisposition toward Yuri—one held by many others in Washington—is what has placed me in this predicament," Fontenot said.

Agent Roman nodded. "Go on."

"When we were at La Gruyère, we joined the chess team. I was hesitant at first but decided to sign up at Yuri's insistence. Playing with some of the best young minds in the world helped me become an avid player as I fell in love with the game. And that has been a bond that I've been unable to break."

"Please explain what you mean by that," Agent Miller said.

"Yuri and I are both very competitive and often ditched our studies for a friendly chess match.

However, they weren't always friendly, often vicious with accompanying bets such as the loser had to streak across campus, oftentimes barefooted in the snow."

"And you continue this tradition today, don't you?" Agent Miller asked.

Fontenot took another gulp from his glass and then placed it back down on the table. "I love tradition, like the kind where we always finish a bottle of vodka while we play a game of chess. And how we made a pact before we left school to meet up once a year for a match and to share what's happening in our lives."

"Is that all that happened?" Agent Roman asked.

"I swear that's it. Just an innocent chess match in Rome one evening that was apparently captured on film by someone who intended to use it against me at some point. I even wore a disguise that night. But someone followed me and took pictures. Now those pictures resurfaced and I appear to be meeting nefariously with Yuri Azarov."

"Is that how the blackmail was presented to you?" Agent Miller asked.

Fontenot nodded. "If I don't resign, these images will be released to the press ahead of my election next year."

"And if we follow the money, where will it lead?" Agent Roman asked.

"I'm not sure, to be honest. Someone obviously wants my seat, though I haven't heard any rumblings from Louisiana about who might be serious about it. I'm nearing the end of my second term, and my approval ratings are through the roof. As the Times-Picayune recently said, I'm 'beloved in the bayou,' which should tell you what you need to know."

Agent Roman scowled. "Just because you're popular with your constituency doesn't mean the opposing party is just as enamored with you. In fact, this is exactly what someone would need to squelch that good feeling and unseat you."

"I know, but as much as I've made my staff keep its collective ear the ground, no one has reported anything about who might be gearing up to challenge me in the upcoming election."

"What about your position as the chairman of the senate intelligence committee? Would someone be angling to steal that from you?" Agent Miller asked.

"Possibly, but I don't know who that would be. We're all pretty good friends—at least all of us on the majority side."

"If you were gone, who would assume your role as Chairman?" Agent Roman asked.

"Well, let's see. I guess that would probably be Senator McWilliams."

"Otto McWilliams, the former CEO of

Pantheon Pharmaceutical?" Agent Miller asked.

"That's the guy, but he wouldn't be behind this," Fontenot said.

"Why not?"

"Otto and I went to Harvard together. We've been friends forever. I even helped him fund the construction of several research labs in Jacksonville when I was working in the finance sector. Our families have vacationed together before. We are together ideologically as any two senators possibly could be."

"Yet *someone* is still pressuring you in an attempt to get either your seat or your power on the committee," Agent Miller said. "Something isn't right. You have to be able to admit that much."

"Of course I can admit that," Fontenot said as he narrowed his eyes. "But the problem is out there somewhere, not on the senate floor and not in Russia. Someone is trying to force me out, and it isn't someone I know."

"I wouldn't be so sure," Agent Roman said. "People never cease to disappoint with their backstabbing ways."

"I'm not that cynical, Agent Roman. I didn't get to this position in life by thinking the worst about everyone I meet."

"Perhaps not, but you won't stay where you are if you don't."

Fontenot stood. "I trust I've given you both enough information to launch your investigation."

"We appreciate your time, Senator," Agent Miller said, offering her hand.

"And I'm grateful for what you do. Just please don't suggest to anyone that I've accused them. I don't want to have to mend fences once this whole ordeal is over."

Agent Roman shook hands with Fontenot. "If mending fences is the extent of the fallout from this situation, you'll be a lucky man. Have a nice evening, Senator."

Fontenot watched the agents walk away and mulled over Roman's parting shot. Maybe he was right. Trusting too many people was never a recipe for success in a city like Washington. But so far, the tactic had served Fontenot well.

He wondered how much time he had before they uncovered the truth.

CHAPTER 4

THE NEXT MORNING, HAWK trudged into the Phoenix Foundation offices and slumped into his chair. He had spent most of the evening researching all of Fontenot's connections and pondering if there was more to the story than the senator let on. Despite nursing a cup of hot tea, he remained groggy and put off by Alex's chipper morning disposition.

"Would you please stop smiling?" Hawk asked.

Alex, sitting directly across from her husband, chuckled at the request.

"You can't even see me," she said. "There are exactly two computer screens between us."

"Doesn't matter," he said. "I know you're grinning like a Cheshire cat—and it's grating on my last ever-loving nerve."

"You only know that because I'm always smiling."

"That doesn't matter—it's still bothering me."

Alex laughed softly. "Someone woke up on the wrong side of the bed this morning, and it wasn't me."

"So, sue me," Hawk said. "I'm grumpy in the mornings."

"More like Godzilla meets King Kong."

Hawk shrugged. "Waking up to your face is always the best part of my day."

"Your flattery won't work on me," Alex said. "I still haven't forgotten that you said I was taking a shower too loud yesterday morning—and I wasn't even singing."

Hawk winced. "I may have blown that out of proportion."

"*May have?*"

"Okay, okay. You win. I definitely blew that out of proportion."

"And?"

"And—I'm—sorry," Hawk said.

"That sounded more like a question than it did an apology," Alex said.

He sighed. "Let me try that again. I'm very sorry, dear. I should've been more sensitive and loving than I was. Will you forgive me?"

"Now that's more like it," she said before focusing on her work again.

"Wait a minute—that's it?" Hawk asked. "I thought—"

"You thought what? That I was going to drop my work for you and tell you that I think you're a swell guy? I love you, Brady Hawk, but you can be a pain sometimes."

Hawk was about to ask her how he could improve when she shrieked. He immediately knew it was the joyful kind as opposed to the horrified shrill noise that emanated from her mouth when she had made an egregious error.

"What?" he asked.

"I think I figured out where these cyber attacks are originating from," she said. "I've been running some algorithms to pinpoint the exact location—and I think I know where it is."

"And?"

"The Changbai mountain range on the border of North Korea and China," she said as she peeked around the side of her computer screen. She was wide-eyed and grinning big.

"And you think we're going there together, don't you?"

She furrowed her brow. "Why not? It's not like going into North Korea would be the most dangerous thing we've ever done."

Hawk bobbed his head in agreement. "You have a point, but we have some logistical issues to consider, starting with how we get in and out of the country. It's much easier with one than two."

She narrowed her eyes while a faint smile

appeared on her lips. "You've become far too protective of me these days. It's like you're my husband."

He winked. "Let's go talk to Blunt about this."

They trekked down the hall to Blunt's office. He was on a phone call but waved them inside as soon as he made eye contact. Mouthing an apology, he pointed at the phone and shrugged.

"Are you sure this trip is necessary?" Hawk whispered. "I mean, can't you just work some of your computer voodoo from here?"

She shook her head. "I'll explain in a minute."

Blunt finally ended his call and exhaled. He set his phone down on his desk and then clasped his hands in front of him.

"So, what have you learned so far?" he asked.

Alex scooted forward in her seat. "Bernard Fontenot is in a bad spot—and there are several perpetrators. But we can't say definitively who's behind it all."

"Sounds like you at least have some leads," Blunt said.

"Well," she started, "there's good news and bad news about that. What do you want first?"

"Dealer's choice."

"I'll start with the good news," she said. "I was able to pinpoint the exact location where the cyber attacks emanated from."

"Excellent," Blunt said. "And where exactly is that?"

"That's sort of the bad news," she said. "Changbai Mountains on the border of China and North Korea."

Blunt sighed. "You have to go there, don't you?"

"Look, my cyber sleuthing can only go so far from here. There are any number of people who could have hired someone in North Korea to administer this assault on the senate's computer system."

"Why couldn't it simply be the North Korean government?" Blunt asked.

Hawk shrugged. "It could be, but that doesn't make much sense. We haven't heard any reports about the North Koreans trying to make a move, especially since there've been overtures of peace in the region. But there are certainly opportunistic people still there who will continue to operate in a country that gladly turns a blind eye to spying on western world powers."

"So you're suggesting these North Korean hackers could be hired by anyone?" Blunt asked.

"Exactly," Hawk said. "For the right price, I'm sure they could resume their operation."

"And you're convinced that's the case?" Blunt asked.

"If you look at who's possibly behind all this,"

Alex began, "the list of suspects is pretty deep—and the North Koreans aren't even really on our radar. And while we're still not certain of the end game, this doesn't seem like something out of the Pyongyang playbook."

"But since these attacks are coming from North Korea, we can't rule them out," Blunt said.

"No, sir," Alex said. "I wouldn't count anyone out at this point. But the intelligence community often rushes to assign blame based on the origin of such an attack, which often seems foolish to me without thoroughly investigating the situation."

"So, suppose I authorize this mission—how do you intend on extracting this information?" Blunt asked.

"Force, intimidation—I don't know," Alex said. "I'm not the expert in such matters, but Hawk is."

Blunt looked over the top of his glasses at Hawk. "Do you have a plan?"

He nodded. "And it's two pronged. Destroy the network to halt the attacks and then coerce the leader to tell me who hired him."

"Those sound more like goals," Blunt said.

"I can get in and get out—and you won't get called onto the carpet on my account for starting some international incident," Hawk said. "You have my word."

Blunt buried his face in his hands. "Why do I think I'm going to regret granting you two permission to do this?"

"Perhaps you've forgotten our stellar record," Hawk said with a grin.

"I haven't forgotten all the headaches, that's for sure," Blunt said before sighing. "Okay, here's the deal. I'll allow you to go, but only Hawk. This mission will be far too dangerous, and I'm certain you can manage from a computer anywhere in the world. You just don't need to go to North Korea to do it. Understand?"

Hawk and Alex both nodded, giving no argument.

"Good," Blunt said. "Now you two get going. We've got to get to the bottom of this ASAP."

CHAPTER 5

Osan Air Base
Pyeongtaek, South Korea

AS THE JET'S TIRES BARKED upon touching down on the runway, Hawk pondered the Phoenix Foundation's tight relationship with the CIA. He had yet to decide if he liked it or not. However, he certainly enjoyed the benefits of traveling abroad when it came to gaining access to most countries. Instead of going through the grueling immigration process with one of his fake passports, Hawk breezed in and out of most locations when landing at a U.S. Air Force base.

Lieutenant Colonel Scott Currant served as the squadron commander at Osan and welcomed Hawk and Alex as they stepped off the plane. Currant ushered them to the special operations room he had set up for the team.

"This mission was supposed to be top secret," Hawk said as they walked. "Do you have personnel who know about what we're doing?"

Currant shrugged. "Everything we do here is on a need-to-know basis. We definitely didn't make any announcement in the base paper, if that's what you're worried about. The only people who know your identity and what you're going to be doing is the pilot we have assigned to take you up for the HALO jump."

"I guess there are some things we just can't avoid, can we?" Hawk asked.

"It's an unfortunate hazard in this business, but I'm sure you're more accustomed to that kind of danger since you're with the CIA."

Hawk preferred to be a ghost when it came to others knowing about what he did. And he felt that way even more so since he married Alex. Their relationship didn't look like most in the agency—one in the field, one chained to a desk—but he still wasn't keen on the idea of others knowing his identity, much less his purpose for being there.

Currant reviewed all of the equipment in the room to make sure that Alex was comfortable with everything. Expressing confidence that she could handle the operation of the technology, she slapped the table and asked about their quarters.

"I do imagine that you might want to rest up before mission launch tomorrow morning," Currant said as he led them down the hall. "No one will bother you in these rooms."

In the east wing of the building, there were about a half dozen hotel-style rooms, all complete with their own kitchenette, stocked pantry, and bathroom. The furniture was modern yet distinctly Asian.

"If you need the cleaning service to come in, let me know," Currant said. "But we try to keep everyone out of this area to give you privacy as well as for your protection. If you need anything, there's a card on the table with my mobile number. Feel free to call me at any time, day or night."

Hawk and Alex both thanked Currant before shutting the door behind him. Once it latched shut, Alex sighed and collapsed onto the couch in a small sitting area adjacent to the bedroom.

"Are we still sure this is the only way to uncover the cyber attackers' identities?" Hawk asked. "Have you exhausted all other means?"

Alex smiled. "Is someone getting cold feet about his HALO jump tomorrow morning?"

Hawk shook his head. "The jump doesn't bother me, but you staying in this place does. We already know that Obsidian has agents everywhere. Who's to say they don't have any already working for them here at base? I prefer we don't talk about this at all, not even in the privacy of this room," Hawk said.

He then put his index finger to his lips before pulling out his pocketknife and removing the cover

over the ventilation duct. Reaching inside, he pulled out a small device about the size of a thimble. Without taking any time to study it, he crushed it with his heel against the kitchen floor. Hawk flipped the faucet on high before speaking.

"This is what I'm talking about," he whispered. "Staying in a random hotel room that nobody suspected we would go to makes me sleep far better at night than being in a place like this that's obviously wired. Who knows how many other cameras there are in this room."

"I'll let you scan the rest of the place while I unpack and get ready," Alex said.

Hawk scurried around the room and didn't find any other signs that they were being watched.

"Coast is clear," he announced once he finished his inspection.

"Permission to speak freely?" Alex asked.

"Permission granted," Hawk said with a wry grin.

She slapped a manila folder into his chest. "Read and memorize everything in that file before your trip in the morning. It's full of good information from the CIA about how to navigate through North Korea and what the best way to connect with the locals is. By the way, how's your Korean?"

"*Aju joh-eunhaji*," Hawk said.

"Not very good? Sounds quite good to me."

"That's only because I've memorized that phrase," Hawk said. "Get me into a conversation and there's no telling what I might say."

"Hopefully that won't be a problem for you and everyone you encounter speaks at least some English," Alex said. "It's the international language of trade—and anyone wishing to deal with Europeans or other powerful people will need to know how to get by with it. If not, use your translator app."

"That's convenient," Hawk said. "I'll be training my gun on a guy while I use my left thumb to type in English words into my phone."

"That's the worst case scenario. I'm sure you'll be fine."

"Okay, let's get some rest," Hawk said. "My flight is supposed to leave at 4:00 a.m. and pre-check starts at 3:00."

"Roger that."

* * *

HAWK WOKE UP a half hour before he needed to be at the hangar. He showered and shaved while preparing himself mentally for the task of parachuting into North Korea. He had performed several HALO jumps before, but he wasn't fond of them. Hawk never thought much of the idea of leaping from a perfectly good airplane at a height of over 20,000 feet and then waiting until the last possible moment to deploy his chute. No matter how competent one was at executing the jump, there were still inherent risks involved. Leaping out of an airplane over the earth with complete faith in a flimsy apparatus wasn't exactly the sport of sane men.

After he was finished getting ready to go, he stopped and stared at Alex as she slept peacefully. He had truly found a woman he could share his life with, every last single piece of it—and he could hardly believe it was real. He thought she looked angelic snuggled up in the bed, causing him to briefly consider easing next to her for a few minutes. But there wasn't time.

He kissed her on the cheek.

"I love you, Alex," he said. "Talk to you soon."

She groaned as she rolled over. "Remind me again why we aren't working corporate jobs like normal people."

"Because neither of us would last a week in a job like that," he said. "Now, I've gotta get going, but I'll see you at the rendezvous point."

Hawk eased out of the room and down the hall toward the exit. As he strode toward the hangar, he tried not to think about what life would be like if they lived like normal people and let some other adrenaline junkies fight the war in the shadows. It was an ideal he dismissed almost as quickly as it came to him.

He's right. I'd hate corporate America.

Upon arriving at the hangar, the pilot, Capt. John Gamble and his co-pilot, Capt. Wade Bullock, reviewed the flight plan with Hawk and shared when and where he would jump in order to hit the target area in the Changbai mountains.

"We have to be extremely careful and keep our altitude high," Gamble said. "We must make sure we don't venture over China and that North Korea doesn't suspect us as a threat, if they see us at all on their radar."

Hawk nodded. "I hear you guys are the best and do this all the time. Is that true?"

"I don't like to brag, but yeah—you won't find any pilots better than us at this," Gamble said. "As long as we don't have any unforeseen complications, you'll be raging like Rambo on those North Korean hackers in no time."

Hawk chuckled and shook his head. "That's not exactly what I do."

"You're not an assassin?" Bullock asked, arching his eyebrows upward.

"I can be if I have to, mostly from long range as a sniper. But I can handle myself in close quarter combat in case you get any ideas."

An awkward silence fell on the room before Hawk broke into laughter and was then promptly joined by the two pilots.

"You had us going there for a minute," Gamble said with a grin.

"I've found it's always good to lighten the mood before such a serious mission," Hawk said.

"Speaking of which," Gamble said, "you'll need to start your oxygen treatment almost immediately after take off. Since you're jumping from twenty-five thousand feet today, you definitely don't want any complications once you land. I'm sure you'll want to hit the ground running—or perhaps killing, whatever the situation requires."

"Sounds good," Hawk said.

Gamble led Hawk to room down the hall where all his equipment was laid out. He suited up and then made his way to the plane, a C-17. The plane's loadmaster, Staff Sgt. Bo Meyer, greeted Hawk and directed him toward the seating area.

"Sit down and make yourself as comfortable as these birds will allow for. No cute skirts to chase or free drinks on board this beast, but it'll get you where you need to go."

"I stopped chasing skirts a long time ago," Hawk said.

"You married?"

Hawk nodded.

Meyer shrugged. "Just because you're married doesn't mean you have to stop looking."

Hawk ignored Meyer's comment, choosing instead to settle onto the rock hard seat. Meyer shuffled away to take care of other pre-flight duties.

Gamble climbed aboard and sought out Hawk.

"You ready?" Gamble asked.

Hawk nodded. "Just give me the word and open up the payload door. I'll take care of the rest."

Gamble flashed a thumbs up. "Did you meet Staff Sgt. Meyer yet?"

"The man who thinks he's Don Juan?"

"Well, that answers my question. Now go get those bastards today and make 'em pay. They're probably the same ones spamming the hell out of my inbox."

The two men chuckled.

"I'm trying to follow your suggestion and keep it light," Gamble said. "I'll let you know when we're going to start depressurization."

"Roger that."

Hawk leaned back in his seat and closed his eyes. He drew in a deep breath and exhaled slowly while imagining all of the details he needed to take care of for the jump. While he rarely got nervous before missions, he felt a little jittery about this one. Plunging toward the earth from such a height was one cause of his anxiety, though he did enjoy the peacefulness of racing toward the ground for a couple of minutes before yanking his rip cord and praying his timing wasn't off. Something just didn't feel right, yet he couldn't put his finger on it.

The flight to the drop zone was just over an hour. Hawk inserted his earpiece and turned it on to see if Alex was already online.

"Good morning, sunshine," Hawk said.

"It won't be until I have my coffee."

Hawk heard the sound of Alex pecking away on her keyboard.

"Is everything operational?" he asked.

"All systems are go. We just need you to fall face first out of the back of an airplane."

Hawk chuckled. "For some reason, I'm not so excited about today's jump."

"Don't worry. If you go splat, I'm sure I'll be able to find some other buff military guy to take care of me."

"That's not funny," Hawk said.

"I'm serious," Alex said. "I can't go back to civilian life now."

"I'm not finding any of these comments amusing."

Alex broke into laughter. "I guess I'm more awake than I thought."

"Your wit apparently doesn't need as much sleep as the rest of you."

"Oh, Hawk. Just stay focused. You'll be fine."

"I know, but something feels off. I can't really explain it."

"You can't make a comment like that and not at least attempt to tell me what you're talking about."

Hawk sighed. "I don't know. There's just this looming sense of danger I have."

"Well, you are—one—jumping out of an airplane from twenty-five thousand feet, and—two—you're landing in North Korea, which is arguably one of our biggest threats militarily right now. So, there's that."

"That's not what I'm talking about, Alex. It's just a sense that something is about to go wrong."

"If there's one person I'd want on the job if things are headed sideways, it's you. You always figure out a way to maneuver through a mess. Always."

"I wish I had as much faith in myself as you have in me."

"It's just that after you've seen it enough times, you start to lose all doubt. How can you even possibly be worried—about anything?"

"Overconfidence can be a killer," Hawk said. "The minute you start thinking you've got it all figured out is the minute you're probably going to die."

Alex exhaled. "I know you're not a negative person, but you sure can transform into Debbie Downer at will."

"I'm not a pessimist—just a realist. It's how I survive."

"Well, shake out the bad feeling before the payload door opens and you begin your walk toward the back of the plane. A feeling won't help you one way or another. You just need to focus on your job and be diligent to look around you at all times to make sure everything is as it should be."

"I'm shaking off the bad feelings right now," Hawk said. "Maybe if you listen closely, you can hear them hitting the tarmac."

The door hummed as it started to rise. Hawk scanned the area and found Staff Sgt. Meyer standing against the wall and holding down a button with one hand while reading an old edition of Playboy in the other.

"They don't make them like they used to," Meyer said before letting out a long whistle. "That is one mighty fine woman."

Hawk rolled his eyes.

"What's the matter with you, pretty boy?" Meyer asked as he stormed over toward Hawk. "Does my lust for women offend you? Are you disgusted by my behavior?"

Hawk shrugged. "Well, now that you mention it—"

"Shut the hell up, you smug self-righteous

sonofabitch. This is my one vice, and I'll be damned if someone like you is going to look down on me for this."

"Just do your job," Hawk said.

"You think I'm a pig, don't you?" Meyer asked. "We all need to roll around in the mud every once in a while. A little dirt never hurt anybody."

Hawk resisted the urge to snap back at Meyer's response. Ultimately, saying anything to him on the subject was meaningless.

Once the door finally latched shut, Meyer marched toward the cockpit to alert the pilots that the back of the plane was prepared for takeoff.

"Let's go, ladies," Meyer said. "It's time to launch this bird into the sky."

A few moments later, the plane turned and then rumbled down the runway. Once Gamble reached the end, he spun the aircraft around and passed along a garbled message over the intercom.

"What's happening now?" Alex asked.

"We're about to take off," Hawk said.

"Good luck," she said.

Gamble accelerated down the runway, the plane collecting speed with each passing second.

The airport seemed to whir by through the windows across from Hawk. Lights flickered past until with a final leap, the plane lurched skyward and climbed steadily up over the city, which was still bathed in the glow of streetlamps.

Once the plane stopped climbing, Hawk initiated his breathing treatment. He went over his mental checklist once again, reviewing all the tasks necessary for the mission to be considered a successful one. The most daunting task would be convincing someone on site to drive him to the coast after he destroyed the hackers' operation. That was the black hole of Hawk's assignment. Waiting on the coast was a fisherman contracted by the CIA to get Hawk to another boat in the Sea of Japan. But it was up to Hawk to figure out a way to get there.

As they neared the jump zone, Gamble alerted Hawk that they were beginning depressurization. It didn't matter much to him since he was already suited up, but it did affect the rest of the crew, which had to switch to oxygen masks in the thin air.

"Approaching the drop zone," Gamble said. "Prepare to jump."

Hawk stood and meandered toward the payload door. Meyer brushed up against Hawk while hustling toward control. Casually, Meyer flipped his middle finger at Hawk, who ignored the juvenile gesture and turned his back on Meyer.

Hawk stared out into the darkness, morning's first light just a few minutes away. Without ever having been in this part of the world, he didn't know what to expect other than what he learned in his briefing. The Changbai Mountains were remote and treacherous, promising a rough landing. But he was ready, even though he had no choice.

The door paused just short of opening fully, causing Hawk to turn around and see what was wrong. When he did, he realized why.

Meyer trained his gun on Hawk and moved slowly toward him. Hawk raised his hands in the air in a posture of surrender and eased away from the payload door and toward a pallet of supplies. But before he could use it as a shield, Meyer wagged his finger.

"That's far enough," Meyer said. "And it's the end of the line for you."

"Captain Gamble, I think we have a problem," Hawk said.

Meyer laughed. "I disconnected your coms earlier."

Hawk didn't wait for Meyer to shoot, diving to the ground and rolling behind the pallet. Thinking quickly, Hawk grabbed the plane's tow bar off the wall and waited for the right moment to strike back. He crouched low and eased to his right, guessing that Meyer would approach from the left.

Hawk took a deep breath and darted around the

side, catching Meyer off guard. The first blow Hawk delivered with the tow bar was to the back of Meyer's knees, knocking him to the ground. The second hit on his arms jarred the gun loose and it slid across the floor toward the back of the plane.

Hawk made a move for the weapon but was surprised when Meyer swung his legs around. After tumbling to the ground, Hawk slid on his stomach a few feet before coming to a stop. Hawk realized that Meyer was headed for the gun and decided to make a more calculated move.

Hawk followed after Meyer, letting him reach the weapon first in exchange for a more advantageous position. As soon as he reached down to pick it up, Hawk slid to the ground and planted both of his feet into Meyer's thigh before giving him a swift push.

Meyer rolled along the sidewall toward the open door, flailing for something to grab ahold of. He managed to get his hands on some cargo netting to stop his slide.

Hawk kicked the gun out of the door and stood over Meyer.

"I'm sorry, man," Meyer said. "I couldn't resist those people. The pay was good, but the job was even better. I was more than willing to take out an arrogant CIA assassin. You were going to jump out the back anyway."

Obsidian is everywhere.

Hawk glanced at the cargo netting and noticed how it was tethered to the airplane. He looked back down at Meyer and wanted to tell him how he definitely wasn't using his brain, but the mask over Hawk's head would've prevented Meyer from hearing a single word in response.

Instead, Hawk pulled the knife from the pocket in his suit and sliced the cargo netting. With one final strand remaining, Hawk looked at Meyer and felt sorry for him. The loadmaster was hanging on for his life and pleading for mercy. And as much as Hawk wanted to extend a hand to the man, he had tried to kill Hawk—and he wasn't convinced Meyer wouldn't try to sabotage the plane after Hawk jumped. Any trust between them was irreparably broken.

Hawk cut the final cord and watched Meyer blow out the back.

Glancing down at his belt, Hawk reattached the cord on his coms, restoring its functionality.

"Hawk? Are you there?" Gambled asked.

"Sorry, I was taking care of some business."

"Okay, well, we're approaching the jump zone," Gamble said. "How are things back there?"

"I was just lightening your load," Hawk said.

"What are you talking about?" Gamble asked.

"Staff Sgt. Meyer is gone."

"What are you talking about?"

"He tried to kill me, but I got the better of him. Maybe you can just fill out in your report that it was an accident or suicide, whatever will give you the least amount of blowback."

"Why didn't you tell us?" Gamble asked. "We could've helped you."

"He disconnected my coms. He also had a gun and you had an airplane to fly. And now I've got a mission to carry out."

"Never liked that guy anyway," Gamble said. "Approaching the drop zone in five seconds."

Gamble initiated a countdown, and when he reached zero, Hawk ran and leaped out of the back.

CHAPTER 6

HAWK ZIPPED TOWARD the ground, hitting a speed of nearly 200 miles per hours. Glancing at the altimeter on his wrist, he realized his fall was going to be a short one. As he neared the 3,500-foot mark, he deployed his chute and guided it toward an open area. Once his feet hit the earth, he ran for a few meters before coming to a stop.

Releasing his harness, he took off his helmet and located a spot in a nearby patch of trees to bury his gear.

"I'm here in one piece," Hawk said over his coms.

"That's a relief," Alex said. "Now that you've done the hard part, all you have to do is fight your way into that facility, destroy the computer system, and then find a way back to the coast."

"Is that sarcasm I detect in your voice, Alex? Because after what I just experienced, that probably was the hard part."

She chuckled. "What do you mean? I was getting a little interference there right before you jumped."

"Is anyone else listening in?" he asked.

"No, just me and you."

"In that case, I can tell you the unfiltered story of how the loadmaster tried to kill me."

Pulling out his GPS to serve as his navigator, Hawk shared all the details of what happened while he walked along the prescribed path.

"Meyer sounded like he got what he deserved," Alex said.

Hawk nodded and stepped over a fallen tree in his path. "It just has me wondering who else Obsidian has coopted to do its bidding," Hawk said. "I'm not sure we've ever run up against a group as dangerous as this. We need to be extra careful about what we say and who we say it to."

"Roger that."

Hawk continued along until he summited a ridge. Crouching low behind a rock, he fished his binoculars out of his pack and scanned the rock face in a small valley below. The only signs of human intrusion into the park that was protected as a wildlife preserve was a dirt road that wound about three miles through the woods and connected with a perpendicular paved road. He waited for a few minutes until he saw a handful of cars as well as two vans rumbling along the path toward a cave. Hawk watched as the caravan stopped briefly before an opening at the base of the rock appeared. The vehicles all drove inside, and the door closed behind them.

"Where did all those cars disappear to?" Alex asked.

"They went inside an opening," Hawk said. "Can you not see that on your feed?"

"The satellite was getting some interference, but the picture's clear now."

"Well, that's where I'm headed now. There's a small door on the side where an armed guard exited a few minutes ago and smoked a cigarette."

"Be careful," Alex said.

"Always."

Hawk hustled down the slope until he came within about fifty meters of the door. Taking cover behind some bushes, he pulled out his binoculars one final time to assess the area. The guard's door had a security pad requiring a thumbprint, and perched overhead was a surveillance camera. Hawk pondered his options.

Using the natural blind, he assembled his rifle and inserted a tranquilizer dart. He wanted to maintain the element of surprise, something that would be lost with a dead security guard. But if he happened to look like he was asleep in his chair, the staff inside might not be so alarmed.

Ten minutes later, the guard came out again for another smoke break. He had finished about half his cigarette before Alex started speaking over the coms.

"What are you waiting for?" she asked. "You need to make your move."

"Common courtesy," Hawk said. "Gotta let the man have his smoke."

With that, Hawk steadied his rifle and then pulled the trigger. The guard crumpled to the ground in a heap. Hawk gathered his gear before racing across the open area toward his victim. Grabbing the man's keycard, Hawk waved it in front of the security panel before he foisted the man's thumb onto the scanner. The door clicked and Hawk tugged it open.

He dragged the guard's body inside, which was a small room covered with video monitors. There was a door leading inside the facility with a window visible from the adjacent corridor.

Hawk propped up the guard in his chair and studied the monitors for a few minutes.

"What are you doing now?" Alex asked.

"I'm inside the security office, and I'm trying to determine where I need to go first," Hawk said.

"I'd suggest finding the server room and then deploying the virus," she said. "That way we can assure these cyber attacks stop. And make sure you get some pictures. I want to see what their operation looks like."

"Roger that."

Hawk peered down the hall and noticed all of the rooms required thumbprints. Working quickly, he removed a kit from his pack and duplicated the guard's print. Armed with the guard's access card, Hawk was ready to get to work.

He hustled down the hallway, stopping at each corner to check for approaching workers. The building traffic was relatively sparse as he only had to avoid a couple workers strolling down the hall.

Peering through the vertical glass slits in each door, Hawk crept through the facility until he reached a room full of servers. He eased inside and wasted no time in uploading the virus to one of the units.

"Alex," Hawk whispered.

"I'm here."

"I found the servers. Anything else you want me to do?"

"As a matter of fact, there is."

She walked through how to relay all the information she needed to hack the servers and download as much information as possible.

"You know if you do that, it's going to trigger a breach alert and this room is going to be swarming with people," Hawk said as he snapped a few pictures.

"Good," Alex said. "It'll save you some time trying to find the people in charge, because you know whoever is running that operation will be one of the first ones in the room."

"I'm not sure that's the best idea."

"Find one of the computers in the back corner, and give me its information," Alex said. "I'll target that one and make it obvious. They'll know exactly which one is being accessed, and they'll try to shut it down first. Then you can lie in wait."

"Fair enough."

"What would you do without me?" Alex asked before quickly adding, "Don't answer that."

Hawk huffed a soft laugh through his nose before following her instructions.

Ten minutes later, footsteps thundered down the hall. Several men stormed into the room and started searching the computers. Hawk peered around the corner of a long row to see if he could determine who was in charge.

One bespectacled man stood at the center of the small crowd, barking orders. After dispensing his commands, all but two men left the room as the others scurried back outside to carry out their assigned tasks. The two remaining men shared a word before the leader marched down the long aisle directly toward Hawk.

"I wouldn't have believed this would work in a million years," Hawk whispered into his coms.

"That's why we're a great team. You've got the brawn, and I've got the brain. It's a formidable combination."

Hawk crouched low and waited for the man to arrive. Once he finally reached the back wall of the room, he headed straight for the computer that Alex had targeted. He placed both hands on the keyboard and started typing, engrossed in his activity.

Hawk seized the opportunity and slipped behind the man, jamming a gun into his back and covering his mouth.

"*Joyonghiiss-eo la*," Hawk said, instructing the man to stay quiet.

The man nodded in acknowledgement.

"Tell your friend to leave the room," Hawk whispered in Korean.

Following orders, the man told the other worker that he could handle the breach on his own. A few seconds later, the door opened and then closed.

"Who are you?" the man asked in English.

Hawk glanced down at the security badge dangling from the man's shirt pocket. Ji-tae Choe was etched just beneath his picture.

"Mr. Choe," Hawk said, "I need your help."

"You haven't answered my question."

Hawk narrowed his eyes. "If you don't answer my question, I'm going to be your worst nightmare.

Now, I'll explain more later if you tell me what I need to know."

"Please, put the gun away," Choe said. "They make me nervous."

Hawk shook his head. "I'm not trying to make you comfortable, but I promise not to use it if you do what I ask."

Choe nodded. "I can't make any promises, but I will do my best. What is it that you want?"

"The names of the people who hired you."

Choe chuckled. "You'll have to be more specific than that. We conduct business for hundreds of clients around the globe."

"We tracked the U.S. Capitol's cyber breach back to your server farm here. Now, who hired you for that job?"

Choe's eyes widened, and he shook his head. "I don't know who you are, but it doesn't matter. Those people are more powerful than you can even imagine. They didn't ask me to do anything—it was a command, the kind that you don't refuse."

"I'm looking for a name, a contact—anything."

"That's not how these people work," Choe said as he wrung his hands. "They send their ghosts in to do their bidding."

Hawk set his jaw. "I don't believe you."

"I swear, I don't know anything."

"Do you have a car?"

The man nodded.

Hawk grabbed him by the arm. "You're going to get me out of here."

Choe poked his head out of the door and checked down the hall in both directions.

"It's clear," he whispered.

Hawk maintained a firm grip on Choe's left bicep. "No games, Mr. Choe. Is that understood?"

With Hawk in tow, Choe eased into the corridor. Using his security clearance, Choe accessed the elevator and descended to the bottom floor. The below ground parking lot was unpaved and rudimentary, utilizing a low-ceiling cave and room enough for no more than a couple dozen vehicles. Beyond that area, there were more boulders and craggy ground that led toward a winnowing tunnel. However, there was light emanating from it.

"Which one is yours?" Hawk asked.

Choe nodded at a van and led Hawk to it. But right as they drew near, Choe stopped and then screamed.

A couple guards had just stepped off the elevator and were now racing toward them.

Hawk dove to the ground and jerked Choe with him. Angling to use Choe as a shield, Hawk tried to drag his captive behind the van and come up with a plan. But Choe grabbed the front tire of the van and held on, rendering Hawk's plan useless. Hawk pistol-whipped Choe, knocking him out before fishing the keys out of his pocket.

The guards fired several shots in Hawk's direction, sending him scurrying behind the back of the van. He tried to put the key into the back to unlock the doors but realized he'd been fooled by Choe. The key fob had the Mercedes-Benz insignia on it.

Hawk cursed his breath as another round of bullets rained down on him. He shoved the key into his pocket and decided that his best bet was to turn the tables on the guards. Instead of being the hunted, Hawk wanted to do the hunting.

He gathered a large rock off the ground and hurled it onto the windshield of a car parked two spaces over. As a result, the car's alarm blared and lights blinked, creating enough of a distraction for Hawk to dart toward the tunnel.

He was nearly to the mouth of it before the guards noticed him racing away. They fired a couple shots that ricocheted off the walls before halting fire.

"Alex! Alex! Where are you?" Hawk asked. "I need your help."

Nothing.

"Come on. Get back to your desk. I'm in serious trouble."

Still nothing.

Hawk couldn't afford to wait for her to answer and give him the information he needed. The guards were sprinting toward him, their footfalls growing louder with each passing moment.

Hawk ran deeper into the cave. "Alex, please answer. I need you."

She didn't respond.

CHAPTER 7

Osan Air Base
Pyeongtaek, South Korea

ALEX'S JOURNEY DOWN the hall to get a cup of coffee was relatively uneventful though hasty. She kept her coms on so she could hear the conversation. While one of the staff sergeants in the break room had on his ear buds, bobbing his head to the beat of his song, Alex was listening to her husband interrogate a North Korean hacker. The other man smiled at her, a gesture she returned before focusing her attention on adding milk and sugar to her coffee. Hawk seemed to have the situation under control, and the captive seemed to be complying.

However, her coms suddenly went out, signaled by a high-pitched squeak that faded quickly. She took it out and inspected it for a moment to see if the power was low. Depressing a button on the cord linking to the two ear pieces, she watched all the green bars flicker on.

That's odd.

She was concerned, but Hawk sounded like he had a firm grasp on what to do next. After doctoring her drink, she hustled down the hallway to her designated room. Her mouth fell agape when she walked in.

Maybe I made a mistake.

She returned to the corridor and checked the nearby rooms.

That couldn't be the right room.

Darting back and forth to check each room, she could feel her heart rate quickening.

Is this some kind of sick joke?

That's when she noticed Lt. Colonel Currant striding down the hallway toward her.

"How are things going?" Currant asked.

The furrowed lines across Alex's brow answered that question well enough.

"I don't know what happened," Alex said. "I just came down the hall to get a cup of coffee, and now all my equipment is gone."

Currant drew back and scowled. "Are you sure?"

"I think so," she said. "Isn't this the room you assigned me to?"

Currant nodded. "That was my understanding."

"Well, it's all gone—every last piece of it, except for these ear buds."

"How could that happen?" he asked.

"That's what I want to know. And right in the middle of the operation, no less."

"There's no way you can get back online?"

"By the time I do, I won't be able to help him. I'm just going to follow the extraction plan and hope that he shows up. At this point, that's all I can do."

"He won't try to contact you another way?"

Alex shook her head. "If he did, it would be via cell phone—and he knows better than to do that, especially in a country like North Korea."

"Where are you headed again?"

Alex eyed him closely. "For security purposes, why don't you get me on a transport plane with enough gas to fly six hundred miles and I'll tell the pilot then?"

"That's not how we work around here. I need to—"

"I can have President Young on the phone in less than five minutes," she said. "Do you want to be on the other end of that call?"

Currant sighed and looked off in the distance, silently pondering the situation.

Alex narrowed her eyes. "It's the least you can do since your security around here is obviously lax."

"Fine. I'll get you your plane. Be ready to go in fifteen minutes."

"I'm ready to go now," she said.

CHAPTER 8

Changbai Mountains
North Korea

HAWK FOUND HIMSELF in a predicament that didn't have any easy solutions. The craggy ground at his feet could prove perilous with the guards bearing down him. But using a flashlight to illuminate his path would also give them a target to aim for. Neither of those options were appealed.

Unable to discern just how many guards were in pursuit forced Hawk to choose a less desirable route. Lying in wait in the darkness could prove lethal to either his pursuers or himself. If there were too many of them, he could be overwhelmed and quickly killed. But two or three seemed manageable. And since Hawk had only seen two men chasing him earlier when there was still light, he decided to take his chances.

Hawk picked his way through the rocks and found a favorable nook to hide in. After shimmying his way inside, he crouched low and waited for the men to pass. One man lit the path while the others all stayed close behind.

Hawk counted the pack hunting him.

One, two, three . . . four.

He wanted to curse but remained silent. The numbers definitely weren't optimal given the conditions. But there wasn't much choice. He certainly couldn't wait out the search as the security team would surely summon more guards to find him. Despite the odds, Hawk still preferred to do the hunting rather than being the hunted.

Once the footsteps faded, Hawk crawled out of his hiding spot and began following the men. He carefully chose his steps before stopping to screw a noise suppressor onto the end of his gun. About thirty meters ahead, the men stopped and began talking in hushed tones.

Hawk knelt down and then took his first shot at the man silhouetted by the shadow of the flashlight he was holding. He let out a cry of pain as he collapsed to the ground. One of the other men reached down and picked up the flashlight. Before he could wield it around the cave and catch the shooter in its beam, Hawk hit the man in the head.

Two down, two to go.

Hawk liked his improving odds, but that changed quickly when two flashlights shone in his direction from opposing sides of the cave wall. He fired at one and then the other, but nothing happened. Hawk quickly realized he'd been duped. The lights had been placed in holes in the cave walls. If the guards were worth their weight in salt, they would now know the direction Hawk was shooting from.

A moment later, darkness returned to the tunnel. Hawk considered spraying the cave with bullets, but it was a calculated risk at best. If he ran out of ammunition, he'd still be at a big disadvantage in the dark of an unfamiliar area with dangerous terrain. And he'd still be outnumbered. Hawk decided to pick his shots and pray he didn't miss.

Hawk stayed low and crawled on his belly toward the men, hoping that they would turn on their lights. A mere second was all the time he would need to take one man out. A few moments later, one of the bulbs flickered on, placing Hawk directly in its beam. He leapt to the side to avoid the light before unleashing several rounds toward it, but it remained on, the holder swaying back and forth before toppling over.

A bullet fired from the other side of the cave and ricocheted off a nearby rock, sending Hawk scrambling. He sought cover behind a boulder and fired another round. The only thing he heard was the sound of the bullet careening off the wall in the distance.

The remaining guard laughed, the echo filling the tunnel. Hawk tried to determine the origin of the noise but struggled. He took one final shot—but he didn't hear a body hitting the rocky floor.

He was out of bullets and wondered if he would have time to reload. The noise would give his position away. But it didn't matter as the remaining soldier charged toward him.

Hawk spun to the side to avoid suffering the brunt of the blow. However, the man had both arms spread wide and was able to corral Hawk before tossing him to the ground. The rocks pounded him on the back, producing a searing pain. Yet Hawk ignored it and continued to move. If he intended to leave the cave alive, he needed to regain the upper hand.

As he spun back toward the center of the cave, footsteps echoed again from behind him. This time, Hawk dropped to his knees, creating an obstacle the attacker didn't sense. He toppled over Hawk and fell headlong toward the ground.

Hawk pounced on him, punching him twice in the face before he swiped at Hawk with a knife. The blade sliced through Hawk's shirt, nicking his chest. He leapt to his feet and edged backward.

By this time, Hawk's eyes had adjusted to the darkness. While he couldn't see everything, he could see enough of the man's faint outline and tell that he was wearing some type of night vision goggles. As the man staggered to his feet, Hawk reached into his pocket and pulled out his flashlight, shining it in the man's face. He winced and tried to shield his eyes, giving Hawk ample opportunity to punch his attacker.

Two more hits sent the man reeling backward. Hawk glanced at the wall to their left and saw several sharp formations jutting out from the side. He blinded the man again before shoving him squarely against one of the pointed edges. The man wailed as the rock pierced his back and came out the front.

Hawk cast his light in the direction of the other men down the tunnel. He saw three dead bodies, yet only two potential uniforms. He sized the men up and picked the one closest in build. A couple minutes later, Hawk sported a guard's uniform and was racing back toward the opening of the cave.

When he reached the mouth, he peered back toward the parking lot. He reloaded his weapon and then spotted Choe, who was just waking up and shaking his head. He grimaced as he looked around and rubbed the back of his neck.

Hawk didn't see any other guards but crouched low as he hustled over to Choe's position.

"How are you feeling?" Hawk asked, training his gun on Choe.

"I'd be feeling a lot better if you hadn't hit me in the back of my head."

"All you had to do was drive me out, but you got some other ideas in that brain of yours. I had to knock some sense back into you."

Choe groaned. "You're not a funny American."

"I'm not trying to be funny. Now, we're going to try this again, only next time it will be a bullet I send crashing into your skull. And I promise you won't like that." Hawk pulled Choe to his feet and ushered him over to his car. "Now, drive," Hawk said, handing the keys to Choe. "Act like nothing's wrong when you pull out of here."

"The guards will know something is wrong. I never leave in the middle of the day under normal circumstances."

"These aren't normal circumstances. You just had a breach—and now you need to meet with someone off site. It's not that hard of a story to believe. But just remember, any false move or signal and I'm going to shoot you in the back."

Hawk climbed into the backseat as Choe settled in behind the steering wheel. They wound their way to the exit near the surface and waited for a guard to open the gate. When he didn't, Choe reached for the visor.

"Watch what you're doing," Hawk said.

"I can leave the garage on my own with this remote," Choe said. "I spend many late nights here, and the guards aren't always awake when I leave. It's the truth—I swear it."

Choe depressed a button on the device and the door to the outside opened up, the bright sunlight overpowering him. He shielded his eyes before putting his car back into gear and easing onto the gas.

After ten minutes, they exited the canyon and found their way to the main road. Choe came to a halt at the traffic light.

"Where do you want to go?" Choe asked.

"Kimchaek," Hawk said without hesitation.

"Kimchaek? That's at least three hours from here."

"Do you need gas money?" Hawk asked before handing over a stack of U.S. one hundred dollar bills. "There's ten thousand U.S. dollars for you."

Choe picked up the cash and smiled as he flipped through the money. He placed it up against his nose and inhaled.

"Ah, the smell of money in the morning," Choe said. "There's nothing like it."

"Well, there's plenty more for you where that came from—if you can help me identify who hired you to initiate this attack on the U.S. Senators."

"I don't know much about him. That's how it is

in this business."

Hawk tossed another stack of bills on the passenger seat next to Choe. "Try to remember."

Choe pulled onto the road and stomped on the gas, the car lurching forward as they sped east toward Kimchaek. "I don't deal with people on a first and last name basis," Choe said. "I only go by their handles on the internet."

"And what was the handle of this particular gentleman who hired you?"

"He went by the name of Undertaker757."

"Remember anything else?"

"Yes," Choe said. "He worked for the U.S. government."

CHAPTER 9

Somewhere in the Sea of Japan

THE YACHT ALEX CHARTERED to pick up Hawk at a rendezvous point in the middle of the Sea of Japan churned through the choppy waters. She directed the pilot Currant assigned for the mission to land on the small island of Ulleungdo. The South Korean territory sat seventy-five miles off the eastern shore of the mainland and served primarily as a tourist destination. Alex thought it was the perfect place to charter a fast yacht without raising an eyebrow.

She borrowed a computer from Currant and attempted to get back online to communicate with Hawk. However, she couldn't get it to function properly. That combined with the spotty satellite coverage in the middle of the water made for a futile exercise.

The captain of the yacht barely spoke any English, though she didn't mind. With all that was going on, she didn't feel like talking to anyone. Her stomach was tied up in knots as she wondered if Hawk was alive or dead. The possibilities of his current state of being rolled through her mind—and she gravitated toward the darkest of places.

They had scheduled to meet at a certain GPS location, agreeing that no ship captain in North Korea would be willing to take them all the way to Japan. The risks were simply too high for anyone commanding a boat out of the communist country. But a short trip off the coast to drop off a passenger for a big stack of money? They both thought their contact on the coast could discreetly sell that idea to at least one willing soul with a seaworthy vessel.

Alex brooded for a few minutes before deciding that she needed to get her mind off the hypothetical and focus on one thing she could do: get the coms working again. She kept tinkering with them until she realized that she needed to tweak one of the channels. Once she did that, her test results came back showing that they were now working properly.

"Hawk, this is Alex," she said. "Do you read me?"

A laugh followed by a shout pierced her ears.

"Loud and clear," he said. "I was beginning to wonder if you had hopped on a flight to Bali and just abandoned me."

"And go cliff diving without you? Where would be the fun in that?"

"I don't know, but I sure am glad to hear your voice. Please tell me that you're on your way to the extraction point."

"We just arrived," she said. "How far away are you?"

Hawk gave her his location and estimated that it would be another hour before they would connect. She exchanged her ship's present course, and they planned to meet along the way.

"What happened?" Hawk asked.

"It's a long story," she said. "I'll have plenty of time to tell you on the way back to the mainland."

"Fair enough," he said.

A little over half an hour later, Alex's boat came upon a fishing vessel floating listlessly in the water.

"Hawk," Alex said over the coms, "are you there?"

He groaned in pain before speaking. "I'm hanging in there."

"What happened?"

"I ran into a little issue with the crew."

"A little issue?" she asked. "What kind?"

"The kind where they want to all kill you. I was just minding my own business below deck when one of these knuckle-draggers walks in and starts yapping at me in Korean. I could barely understand him but got the message loud and clear when he pulled out a knife and started pointing at my bag. I pinned him against the wall, knocking the weapon out of his hand before I tied him up. But that wasn't all."

"There's more?"

"I'm only getting started," Hawk said. "Then two more guys returned, this time armed with guns, but I was ready. I shot both of them, which drew the attention of a couple of other sailors who were milling around on the deck. They came after me as well."

"So, what's happening right now?"

"I'm sitting in my quarters, reading a book, and praying that the anchor would keep me from drifting too far off course."

"You had to take out the captain, too?"

"Apparently he was the ring leader," Hawk said. "But at least I got all my money back."

"Well, steady the ship because I'm about to come aboard and get you."

"That's not necessary."

"I didn't give you an option."

Alex hustled outside and then tied off a rope along the top of the fishing boat's deck. She secured the cord to the yacht and climbed up to Hawk's vessel. Hawk stood in the doorway leading down the stairs to the hull. He was leaning against the side and grinning.

"You've always wanted to rescue me, haven't you?" Hawk asked.

She strode up to him and gave him a hug and a kiss.

"This isn't the first time I've done this, you know," she said, punctuating her remark with a wink.

Hawk furrowed his brow. "You'll have to refresh my memory about the other time this happened."

"Other *times*," she said. "If it wasn't for my quick thinking, you might still be drifting along out here, hoping that someone would come along and pick you up."

"If you hadn't abandoned me on the coms when I really needed you, I may not have been in such a dire situation in the first place."

Alex chuckled. "Just change the subject or deflect—that's one way to move off the topic. But, for the record, my equipment was stolen on base. I would *never* abandon you."

"Stolen?" Hawk asked as he stopped and looked skyward.

"What is it?" Alex asked.

"They're coming for us," he said, rushing toward the edge. "We need to get the hell outta here."

"Who's coming for you?"

"The North Koreans," Hawk said, scanning the horizon. "That's one of their jets screaming this way."

"Are you sure?" Alex asked.

Hawk continued to peer out across the water. "I'm positive."

"And how would they know where you are?"

Hawk frantically searched his pockets and after a few seconds dug out a small device about the size of a collar button.

"This," he said, holding up the device. "Choe must've slipped it into my jacket somehow. Maybe when we stopped to get gas and I had to use the bathroom. I bumped into him. That could've been when he did it. At the time, I thought it was simply awkward."

"Apparently, it was far more than that."

After placing the tracker down, Hawk finally looked back up before identifying the jets, which banked hard to the right before heading straight toward them.

"We need to get out of here right now," he said.

They scrambled over to the other boat and implored the captain to open up the throttle and move as quickly as possible, but he was barely awake, nursing a bottle of whiskey.

"We need to go now," Hawk said.

With eyes glazed over, the man stared at Hawk.

"What?" the captain asked, barely coherent. "What's happening?"

Hawk grabbed the man's bottle and tossed it into the water. After pushing the man out of the way, Hawk shoved the throttle forward. The boat slowly built speed as he tried to put more distance between them and the other vessel.

"Come on, come on," he said.

He checked over his shoulder again and watched as the two North Korean fighter jets lined up with the fishing boat and dropped low, no more than a hundred feet above the water. Hawk could hardly breathe as the planes obliterated the other vessel. Shards of wood zipped through the air in every direction, escaping a fireball at the center of the hull. Hawk said a little prayer as the jets roared overhead. He watched as they banked west and then turned all the way around, this time heading straight toward the yacht.

Alex looked at Hawk. Her eyes seemed to beg for a shred of hope, which was something he was in short supply of.

"If they hit us——" she said.

"I know, I know," Hawk said.

"Well, do something."

The only way Hawk could do something meaningful would be to pull out an RPG and light up the planes. Anything else he did would just be to make himself feel better. And that was an empty gesture given the circumstances.

Hawk turned the ship east and carefully watched the skies above to see how the jets responded. They both maintained their original flight pattern.

After taking one more pass over the wreckage, the jets lit their afterburners and took off toward the mainland.

Hawk exhaled and looked at Alex, who was wide-eyed.

"That was too close," Alex said.

"Yes, but we're still alive—and that's what really matters. And I also have the handle of the perpetrator, so it couldn't be much better, to be honest."

"Dodging North Korean fighters in the Sea of Japan? It can get much better than this."

The ship's captain stumbled toward Hawk again.

"This is my boat," the man said, slurring his words. "Why are you in the captain's seat?"

"We needed to get the hell outta there—and you were smashed on something," Hawk said. "And from the looks of it, you still are."

"I'm fine," the captain said emphatically. "Now let me take us home."

"Not on your life," Hawk said before cold cocking the man.

He stumbled backward and then crumpled to the deck.

"Where did you find this guy?" Hawk asked Alex.

"He came with the boat," she said. "I wasn't too concerned at the time since he wasn't drunk when we started out."

"Never trust a man who names his boat *Wild Turkey*," Hawk said. "Now let's get back to work. We've got a lot to do if we're going to put a stop to this threat."

CHAPTER 10

Osan Air Base
Pyeongtaek, South Korea

THE SHORT FLIGHT back to the base from Ulleungdo was spent rehashing the details of what went wrong for both Hawk and Alex. However, Hawk wasn't crazy about returning to Osan and warned Alex against saying anything about the details of the operation to anyone, even Lt. Col. Currant. With Obsidian having infiltrated a U.S. outpost in South Korea, Hawk grew increasingly uncomfortable when he considered just how wide reaching the organization's network was.

"Do you think Currant was behind any of this?" Alex whispered in an effort to maintain a low profile and keep the pilot from eavesdropping.

"We can't rule out anyone at this point," Hawk said. "Not even Currant, even as much as I like him."

As they circled the landing field, the lights below winked in the early evening darkness. The tires chirped as the plane landed before the pilot navigated the aircraft to a nearby hangar. Currant was waiting for them with his hands clasped in front of him. As soon as Hawk and Alex exited the aircraft, Currant hustled up to them.

"You made it back in one piece," Currant said. "Must've been a successful mission."

"I heard things got a little weird here," Hawk said, ignoring Currant's leading statement. "Have you been able to review any surveillance footage and figure out who stole all of Alex's equipment?"

"We're still working on that," Currant said. "As you know, these security systems are designed to be difficult for people to hack. We're doing the best that we can to figure out how this hapened."

"They might be difficult to hack, but they should be simple to review for people who have all the right access codes," Alex said.

"That's right, but we still haven't located them. Two members of our team are at a security conference today, and the other one holding down the fort went home sick this morning. We've been unable to reach him since."

"That sounds suspicious," Hawk said. "Who is this guy?"

"It's a woman, actually," Currant said. "Lyla Givens is her name, but we'll handle it on our end. I'm sure there's a reasonable explanation for all of this."

"Perhaps, but it seems like you have a mole in your midst," Hawk said. "Entire computing systems don't just manage to vanish into thin air by accident."

"I promise you that we'll get to the bottom of this."

"We appreciate that," Alex said.

"Is there anything else I can do for you?" Currant asked.

"Just let our pilot know that we need to prepare for departure within the next ninety minutes," Hawk said.

Currant clapped his hands and rubbed them together. "I can definitely handle that. Want me to tell him where to file flight plans for?"

"We'll tell him ourselves," Hawk said, extending his hand to Currant. "We appreciate your hospitality here."

"Any time," Currant said, shaking Hawk's hand then moving to Alex. "Sorry about the mishaps, but I'll let you know once we've located your equipment. I'm sure it was just a miscommunication of sorts."

Alex nodded knowingly before she and Hawk turned around and headed back toward the hangar.

"We need to call Blunt," Alex said.

"I'm not calling anyone until I'm outside and sure that no one is listening," Hawk said.

They marched across the tarmac in silence while planes both rocketed skyward and roared along the runway after touching down.

The brief break in conversation gave Hawk a chance to think. He wasn't sure if Currant was simply trying to be helpful or if he had designs on sabotaging them. If Obsidian's web stretched far and wide across the globe, a base commander on the organization's payroll wasn't a farfetched idea.

They walked about fifty meters behind the hangar to buffer the noise before placing a call to Blunt. Hawk put the audio on speaker so Alex could listen in. Blunt grunted as he answered the phone.

"We're calling to give you an update on the latest operation," Hawk said.

"You don't have to," Blunt said. "I already know it was a success."

"Who told you that?" Alex asked.

"I got a call from the security team over at the Capitol Building," Blunt said. "All the attacks originating from North Korea suddenly stopped earlier today. I'm assuming you had something to do with that."

"We did," Hawk said. "It wasn't easy though."

Blunt chuckled. "It never is, is it?"

"Most definitely not," Alex said. "I even had to deal with the loss of all my equipment during the middle of the operation."

"What happened?" Blunt asked.

"It's a long story, and, to be honest, we still don't know all the details. But in short, my computer and all my other electronic equipment was stolen."

"Can you wipe the hard drive remotely?" Blunt asked.

"I already initiated that protocol through a backup web portal," Alex said.

"I look forward to a full report when you return, but I'm glad you called because I need to talk to you about another operation."

"What now?" Hawk asked. "Did you get any other leads from the Orlovsky contacts?"

"No," Blunt said. "But I did receive intel that Admiral Adelman is in Hong Kong for a meeting with members of Obsidian. Apparently, a large number of their mid-level and upper-level leadership will be in attendance."

"This ought to be an interesting reunion," Hawk said. "I'm sure my former Navy SEAL commander will be surprised to see me."

"Adelman has a lot to answer for."

"So we're going to crash the party?" Hawk asked.

"In a manner of speaking, yes," Blunt said. "It's probably going to look a little different than most of your other missions."

"How so?"

"I want you to enter through the front door with everyone else," Blunt said.

"And how exactly would we do that?"

Blunt exhaled loudly. "Do you remember when we started Firestorm and I told you that there were three assassins that I kept on that team?"

"I remember you saying that, but I only remember meeting one other one—the one I had to kill," Hawk said.

"Your path never crossed with the third assassin, who worked alone on cases that required a smaller footprint and more discretion," Blunt said.

"Who is he?"

"His name is Titus Black, and he's been working deep undercover for quite some time, trying to infiltrate a dangerous shadow organization. When he started, we didn't know the name Obsidian, but now we know that's the group he was tracking."

"So, Black can get us into this meeting?" Hawk asked.

"Yes, he tentatively arranged for you to accompany him as an illegal arms seller, all predicated on your ability to get to Hong Kong in time, which now you'll be able to make if you don't delay."

Hawk took a deep breath and stared off in the distance. He hated the idea of working with someone other than Alex, especially after getting burned so many times in the past.

"How come I've never met Black?" he finally asked.

"Just play nice, okay?"

CHAPTER 11

Hong Kong
Victoria Harbor

THE NEXT AFTERNOON, Hawk leaned on the railing and peered out over the ships chugging through the busy harbor. On his right, Alex stood with her back to the scene, scanning the area in the opposite direction. A stiff wind tousled their hair and caused Hawk's eyes to tear up.

"Usually it's the ladies who cry when they see me," a man said in a low voice to Hawk.

Turning to his left, Hawk looked over to see a bulked-up man sporting sunglasses and a blue baseball cap.

"You're not nearly as handsome as Blunt described you," Hawk said.

Black smirked. "He does like to oversell, doesn't he?" He turned toward Alex. "And this young woman must be Alex, the lady with the magic touch."

Hawk put his right hand on Black's chest and

pointed at Alex's wedding band with his left. "Don't get any ideas," Hawk said. "She's spoken for."

Black raised his hands in a gesture of surrender. "Just repeating what I heard. We're all on the same team here. No need to get testy."

If Hawk could've swung and knocked out Black and still been admitted to the secret Obsidian meeting, he would have. But he decided to heed his colleague's suggestion.

"In that case, let's talk about tonight," Hawk said. "Tell me what I need to know about attending this gathering."

"It's more like an auction than anything," Black said. "We'll be seated around a long table, and various buyers will parade their wares in front. Obsidian is hosting the event because they're seeking certain services and commodities. However, they have positioned themselves as a bridge between buyers and sellers of various illegal activities."

"Sounds like we'll have a motley crew on hand."

"You'll be surprised at the clientele in attendance. These are not low-life knuckle draggers from third world nations. There are respected businessmen along with former military leaders and ambassadors. You'll even find powerful women there, too. This group is networked across the globe. And while they're not all officially part of Obsidian, they will do favors for the organization from time to time."

"From what you're saying, this could be our chance to wipe out a large number of evil leaders in one fell swoop."

Black shook his head. "That's a good idea in theory, but in reality we would simply lose our ability to follow these networks and see how they're being funded and where all the connections are. Besides, we don't even know where the meeting is yet."

"Did we fly to Hong Kong for nothing?" Alex asked.

"No, the meeting *is* here, but we won't know exactly where until later tonight," Black said. "The process of finding out the location is shrouded in secrecy. A half-hour before the meeting, we receive coordinates via text message about where we should go. Upon arriving at the location, we must surrender our phones before receiving a slip of paper with another address. Once we arrive there, we'll be personally escorted to the actual site."

Hawk nodded. "That protocol would certainly make it difficult to strike the location."

"Exactly," Black said. "There's also a state-of-the-art metal detector along with a pat down to make sure there aren't any weapons in the room. We can't go in with our guns blazing, especially if we're going to apprehend Adelman for questioning."

"What are your plans for interrogating him?" Hawk asked.

"I'll follow Adelman out when he exits for a bathroom break. Once there, I'll ask him a few questions and see what he has to say about his meeting with the Chinese."

"That sounds like a terrible plan," Hawk said. "Because you'll be in a public place devoid of weapons, he will stonewall you—and he can get away with it since you're not in a private area. Adelman trained the best of the best. He also served as a SEAL. He knows how to manipulate the situation. You're going to need to do more to him than simply ask him a few questions in the men's room."

"What do you suggest then?" Black asked.

"I think we need to take him somewhere, a place where we can make the kind of threats he will cower to. Then we need to question him properly, expressing the kind of urgency we have regarding this situation. If he doesn't respond to that, we can move on to more persuasive means."

"I'm afraid that just isn't going to happen," Black said. "I need to maintain my access to the group, which means we'll have to work more slowly than perhaps you're accustomed to. The end goal is to get information out of Adelman in a way that preserves my standing with them."

Hawk shook his head. "If I'm hearing you correctly, I find those two goals to be mutually exclusive. We're not going to find out what we need to know if you're trying to tread lightly in approaching Adelman. A full-throated interrogation is the only thing Adelman is going to respond to in a manner that gets us what we need."

Black furrowed his brow as he removed his sunglasses. "Let's get one thing straight here, Hawk. I'm in charge of this operation. You're going to do what I need you to do. And if that's standing in the shadows while I try to make contact with Adelman, then that's what you're going to do. If you don't like this arrangement, you can take it up with Blunt. He's the one who charged me with handling this operation. You're only here for support. Got it?"

Hawk sighed and then nodded. "Apparently, you're the boss. Just tell me where I need to go so I can stand there and look pretty."

A wry grin leaked across Black's face. "Now you're starting to get it."

* * *

HAWK ADJUSTED his fake glasses before straightening his tie.

"How do I look?" he asked Alex.

She shrugged. "Not bad considering all that you've been through in the past forty-eight hours."

"I'll take that as a great compliment then."

Alex shook her head. "I just don't want you to look any worse when you return later tonight."

Hawk furrowed his brow. "What do you mean by that?"

"You know exactly what I'm talking about—you and Black. It's quite evident that you two aren't won't be fly fishing together on the South Fork of the Salmon River in your down time."

"I wouldn't be doing that on my own during any vacation time."

"True," she said, batting some dust off the shoulders of his sports coat. "You'd be doing it with me."

"Since when did you get into fly fishing?" Hawk asked.

"Just because you're married to me doesn't mean you know everything about me—yet. But by the time we're old and gray, you better know how many millimeters the mole on my left shoulder blade is."

"Six," Hawk deadpanned. Unable to hold his straight face for more than a few seconds, he cracked a big grin.

"Good guess, but wrong. However, we have a lifetime to learn every little thing about one another. And that lifetime I'm referring to better be a long one."

Hawk shrugged. "Well, when you married me, you knew what you were getting yourself into."

"I also know that you better control your impulsiveness," Alex said. "We need to work with Black, not undermine him."

"I would never—"

"Just stop right there," she said as she held up her right hand, palm flat and just a few inches from his face. "I know how you are, which is why I'm saying this. Play nice. Understand?"

Hawk nodded. "You sound just like Blunt."

"That's because we both know you so well."

"Fine. I'll be on my best behavior. But at the end of the day, we need answers, and if Black can't get them—"

Alex pressed her forefinger against Hawk's lips. "Just go do your job. And remember that I'll be able to communicate with you and see everything you see as long as you have those glasses on."

"Roger that," he said before hugging Alex.

A knock on the door interrupted their embrace. Hawk peered through the peephole and saw Black. Opening the door, Hawk gestured for Black to join them.

"It's time to get going," Black said. "I just received the text."

Hawk kissed Alex on the cheek.

"We'll be in touch," Black said to Alex.

"I'll meet you at the CIA warehouse later tonight," she said.

* * *

AN HOUR LATER, Hawk and Black stood inside the first floor of a stark department store that was still under construction. Opaque plastic sheets hung from the rafters and served as makeshift walls. A cool breeze rustled them as Hawk and Black followed a man to the back of the building. He led them into an alley where a car was waiting. Before he permitted them to pass, he requested all electronic devices be deposited into the basket he held. Black obliged while Hawk gestured that he didn't have any. After a brief pat down, Black and Hawk were allowed into the vehicle.

They wound around the streets of Hong Kong for fifteen minutes before disappearing into a tunnel. When they reemerged, they drove along another few blocks and then turned into a parking deck. The driver took them down several floors well below ground, braking in front of a set of doors.

A man in a tuxedo stationed outside the entrance hustled over and opened the car door for his guests. He then ushered them onto an elevator and inserted a key before depressing the button that took them to the bottom floor. Hawk wasn't certain what floor they'd started on, but they descended for another minute. Once they stopped, the door slid open and Hawk was taken aback by the festive atmosphere inside the large room in front of him.

Pulsating music thumped on the loud speakers as black lights flashed. A scantily clad waitress breezed past him, pausing briefly to offer a drink. Hawk politely declined and turned his attention elsewhere.

"Are you always that quick to look away?" Alex asked over the coms.

Hawk smiled and nodded subtly. He scanned the rest of the room and saw several rows of chairs set up near a podium in the far corner of the room. Large monitors hung from the ceiling, and a countdown had already been initiated. It showed there were less than three minutes remaining. Hawk wasn't sure what would happen when zeros hit, but he assumed that would signal the beginning of the meeting.

The people in the room, mostly comprised of men, moved around in pairs and rarely interacted with others.

"Is this how all their meetings are?" Hawk asked Black.

"This is a little out of the norm," Black said, "but by and large, this is what I saw the only other time I wormed my way into an Obsidian marketplace meeting. Half-naked women offering free alcohol to clients, techno music, and a less than cordial atmosphere."

"So, it's not just me?" Hawk asked.

"These clients barely trust their own assistants, let alone anyone else."

Hawk growled. "That's going to make it quite obvious when you approach Adelman."

"It may not matter," Black said. "I haven't seen Adelman here yet."

Hawk glanced at the clock showing just under two minutes remaining. "I suppose there's still time."

"But if he does show up, you're right. I'm going to have to tread carefully if you expect to get any information out of him. That's why you're going to watch the door for me."

"Won't he have someone watching the door for him?" Hawk asked.

"Maybe, but you know what to do in a case like that."

Hawk and Black continued to study the rest of the clientele while waiting for the meeting to begin. Along with over a dozen men dressed in suits, there were sheiks adorned in traditional Middle Eastern garb, a woman in a pantsuit, two men wearing African tribal attire, and four men sporting camouflage gear.

"If I didn't know any better, I'd think we were at some comic-con event," Hawk said.

"Just give it a minute," Black said. "Batman will stride through the doors any second now."

"Aren't you two just regular comedians," Alex chimed in over the coms.

Hawk and Black both turned and looked toward the entrance at the same time. The elevator doors slid open, and three more guests spilled out.

"Well, it's not Batman," Hawk said, "but it is who we came here for."

Admiral Adelman walked casually into the room, his hands thrust deep into his pants pockets. He wore a three-piece suit accented with a golden chain attached to what Hawk could only assume was a pocket watch. Adelman's suit was tailored and showed off his chiseled frame. He may have trained Navy SEALS for several years, but Hawk could tell his former supervisor was still in top shape. He was also attending alone.

The clock on the monitor struck zero, and an alarm whooped over the speakers. Immediately, the black lights were exchanged for more suitable house lighting while the music quickly faded out. A man holding a microphone stepped onto the stage and urged everyone to join him in the main meeting area. He enthusiastically expressed how excited he was to begin the evening's festivities and wasted no time in showcasing the first item on the docket.

"Fresh off the boat from Galveston, Texas, we have a dozen Personal Ultrasonic Ballistics—or PUB-47s," the man said. "These state-of-the-art weapons come here compliments of Colton Industries and will enable your small band of vigilantes to level the playing field against a corrupt government trying to snuff out your resistance. The bidding begins at two hundred and fifty thousand dollars. Do I have any takers?"

Hands went up all around the room. Black's hand shot up as he bid early and often, driving the item's cost up to well over two million dollars before bowing out. A Middle Eastern man pumped his fist after being declared the winner of the auction.

"Now those Americans will have to worry about more than just a roadside IED," the man said as he rushed over to the table just off to the side of the stage to make payment arrangements.

Hawk leaned over and whispered to Black. "This is insane. Those weapons were stolen, no doubt about it."

"And you think anyone here cares about that?" Black asked.

"Of course not, but it's scary how easily these maniacs can get their hands on powerful weapons."

"This kind of buying and trading has been going on for years," Black said. "There's nothing new about any of this, except maybe the fact that you're here to witness it all. But just you wait; you haven't seen anything yet."

The emcee continued by introducing the next item. "This next one comes all the way to us from Hiroshima, Japan—six skillfully trained ninjas who specialize in kidnapping."

"Wouldn't you like to meet that crew in a back alley?" Black joked.

"Not without a weapon," Hawk said, tapping his coat pocket.

Black's eyes widened. "You snuck a gun in here? Are you crazy?"

"Given what I've seen in the first five minutes of this gathering, I think bringing a gun in here was about the most sane decision I could've made."

"How did you get that in here anyway?"

"My wife is good at printing guns," Hawk said. "This one can even hold six shots."

"You better not use it. Six shots won't be enough."

"Don't get your panties in a wad," Hawk said. "I'm only shooting tranq darts."

Black narrowed his eyes. "We're doing this my way. Do you understand?"

"By all means, do your thing," Hawk said. "I'm just here to look pretty, remember?"

The next half hour of the auction saw everything from rocket launchers to missiles up for sale as well as the services of elite assassins. With the room full of highly trained killing machines, Hawk considered how unlikely it'd be to escape alive. He also kept an eye on Adelman, who'd yet to raise his hand to bid on anything.

After declaring a winner for two long-range ballistic missiles, the emcee adjourned for a fifteen-minute break. The black lights returned as did the pulsating music. Hawk watched as Adelman headed straight toward one of the women offering drinks. He grabbed a tumbler filled with bourbon and downed it without hesitation.

Adelman always could drink like a fish.

Hawk watched as his former training supervisor traded the empty glass for another full one, draining the liquid in a matter of seconds, too. After one final swap, Adelman meandered back toward his seat but was stopped when he was blocked by Black.

Hawk could hear the conversation loud and clear on his coms.

"Hi, Admiral," Black said. "We need to talk. Don't you need to use the restroom?"

Adelman didn't budge. "I'm sorry, sir, but do I know you?"

Black shrugged. "We're about to become plenty acquainted."

"I'm not going anywhere with you," Adelman said. "All I need to do is alert security that someone is threatening me, and you'll be tossed out of here fast—and likely in a body bag."

"Go ahead and alert them" Black said. "What's stopping you?"

"Just move out of my way so I can get back to my seat," Adelman said. "I promise you that you don't want to tangle with me."

Black didn't flinch. "You need to talk with me right now."

"Maybe your hearing is bad after getting beaten so often, but I'm only going to say this one more time before I notify the security team here about your threat."

"Be my guest," Black said. "You're the impostor here, not me."

Before Adelman could respond, he slumped to the floor.

"What the hell," Black said, scanning the room.

Hawk slipped the gun back into his coat pocket and watched Black discreetly remove the dart before calling for medical help from the security staff. A trio of men hustled over toward Adelman and knelt on the ground to inspect him. One man put on gloves and checked Adelman's vitals. Satisfied that there wasn't anything he could do with his immediate findings, he lifted up Adelman's eyelids and shone a light on them.

"What happened?" the man asked Black.

"I don't know. One minute we were having a conversation. The next he simply fell to the ground. It was the strangest thing."

"It couldn't be a heart attack. His pulse is strong and normal for a man about his age."

Another security member joined them.

"Do you know this man?" he asked.

Black nodded. "I'll take him to a hospital and get him the medical attention he needs."

A small crowd had gathered by this point, mostly to inspect what had happened and likely to determine if there was any immediate threat on their own lives. The emcee put his hand on Black's chest.

"You don't have to go," the emcee said. "We have plenty of experienced professionals who can give this man all the care he requires."

"I want to go with him," Black said. "This man has been a friend of mine for a long time."

"But we haven't even given out tonight's gifts for all those in attendance," the emcee protested. "Everyone here will need one when we move into phase two next week."

Hawk didn't twitch his facial muscles while speaking into his coms.

"Are you getting all this, Alex?" he asked.

"Loud and clear," she said. "I just switched us to a private channel. Looks like you're going to have fun getting out of there."

"I don't like not being included in this," Hawk said.

"Of course you don't. But Blunt trusts this guy—and we should too."

Hawk continued to watch the scene unfold as heard a strange sound in the background.

"What was that, Alex?"

"Well, that's interesting," she said. "Are you still keeping an eye on the situation?"

"Yeah, but I can't see too much because more people have crowded around them. It's like a mosh pit over there."

"I'm glad you have eyes on him because his signal just went dead."

"What the—"

"Yeah, you heard me," Alex said. "Does Black still have his glasses on?"

"Give me a second," Hawk said as he strode across the room to get a more favorable angle on Black. After a few seconds, Hawk was able to see his partner's face.

"I don't see his glasses anywhere," Hawk said.

"I'm sure there's a reasonable explanation for that, but stay close just in case."

"Roger that," Hawk said.

Scanning the room once more, he walked over toward the far wall and leaned against it. Someone inside the circle was yelling for the house lights to be turned back on. Hawk watched a man scurry across the room in response to the request. If there were security cameras, they wouldn't be able to detect much of anything without proper lighting. Hawk glanced to his left and then his right before reaching for the fire alarm and yanking it hard.

He dashed away from the wall and casually picked up a drink off a tray abandoned on a nearby table by one of the waitresses. The room fell into an uproar, and panic ensued. Hawk wormed his way over toward the group huddled around Adelman. The alarm blared, and red lights flashed over the exits.

"We need to get out of here now," Hawk whispered in Black's ear.

Hawk looked down and noticed the glasses crushed on the floor next to Black's foot.

"I found the schematics for this building online and looked up another exit for you," Alex said over the coms.

"You take the lead," Hawk said as he helped up Adelman. Black and Hawk each grabbed one of Adelman's arms and slung it around their necks so they could drag him.

"We'll take care of him," Hawk said to one of the security guards, who shrugged and didn't question them any further.

The chaos in the room over the fire alarm sent everyone scurrying for the exits, allowing Hawk and Black to head down a long corridor without being noticed. They entered a stairwell and trudged upward.

"How many flights do we need to go, Alex?" Hawk asked.

"Ten."

"Ten flights it is," Hawk said.

"We have to cart this guy up ten flights of stairs?" Black asked.

"Unless you'd like to have the honor of doing it on your own, we're going to do this."

"What kind of tranq did you hit him with?" Black asked. "Is he going to be out long?"

"We've probably got another fifteen minutes before he comes to. So, in the meantime, maybe you can tell me why you took your glasses off and stomped on them?"

Black scowled. "I didn't take them off. One of the security guys hit me with an elbow while attempting to tend to Adelman."

"Likely story," Hawk said with a sneer.

"Remember, Hawk—play nice," Alex said in his ear.

"It's the truth," Black said. "We're supposed to be a team, although you didn't help matters by making a unilateral decision to knock out Adelman with your gun that you weren't supposed to bring inside."

Hawk shrugged. "This seems to be working out."

"What do you think's going to happen when we surface on street level?" Black asked. "We're just going to lug Adelman around Hong Kong like *Weekend at Bernie's*?"

"That—or we could call an Uber," Hawk replied.

"That'll be difficult since they took our phones."

"Not with Alex on hand," Hawk said. "She'll order one for us since she has a tracker on us and knows exactly where we are."

"I'm on it," Alex chirped in Hawk's ear.

Black shook his head. "You got lucky this time. But don't ever go rogue with me again. We need to act like a team."

"Standing in the corner and looking pretty isn't my idea of how a team operates," Hawk said. "If we're going to work together, we need to *work* together."

"You're impeding on my turf and could've seriously screwed up my operation."

"Well, you can thank me later for this," Hawk said. "I didn't blow your cover, and we're about to get a whole hell of a lot more information out of Adelman while interrogating him in an environment we control than in some random men's restroom."

Just as they reached the landing on the street level, Adelman moaned and opened his eyes.

"What happened?" he asked. "Where am I?"

"Hang on," Hawk said. "I've got another tranq."

Black drew back and punched Adelman in the face, knocking him out cold.

"What'd you do that for?" Hawk asked.

"I thought you'd appreciate that," Black said. "Sometimes you just have to improvise, don't you?"

CHAPTER 12

HAWK SPLASHED WATER on Adelman's face in an attempt to bring him back to consciousness. With eyes closed, he screwed up his face and writhed against the ropes binding him to a chair in the stark room deep in the belly of a CIA black site in Hong Kong. Slowly he opened one eye and then the other before a hard scowl spread across his face.

"Brady Hawk?" Adelman asked with a growl. "What's the meaning of all this? What are you doing to me?"

"I'll be the one asking the questions this time," Hawk said as he circled Adelman.

"You're making a big mistake," Adelman said.

"It seems to me that you've already made one in the way you choose your friends."

"I can promise you that looks can be deceiving—and certainly are in this case."

Hawk stopped in front of Adelman and stooped down to get eye level. "That's hard to believe. I remember when we were in training, you drummed into our heads that whenever you're taken captive, you say anything to gain your captor's trust."

"You're forgetting one important element—keep everything as close to the truth as possible. Once you start telling lies, you're bound to make a mistake somewhere along the way."

"So I should just believe whatever you say?" Hawk asked.

"I swear that whatever reason you have for holding me like this, it's a mistake."

"Why? Is someone going to come looking for you?"

Adelman nodded. "Maybe the U.S. government."

Hawk shook his head. "Right now, I am the U.S. government. And your only chance of getting out of here is if you tell me the truth about why you've been colluding with Obsidian."

"If you're employed by the government and you've captured me like this, I know you're acting on your own."

Hawk clapped slowly and then crossed his arms. "I must say that your performance has been outstanding up until this point, perhaps even somewhat plausible. But I know the truth."

"You know nothing of the truth when it comes to my dealings with Obsidian."

"Enlighten me."

"What did you think? That I'm one of their stooges?"

"All the evidence points in that direction. We've got all kinds of evidence that documents such a relationship—secret bank accounts where you've been stashing loads of cash along with your name surfacing on a list of contacts from Russian arms dealer Andrei Orlovsky. It's all quite damning. And then here you are at a gathering like this."

"Use your brain, Hawk. I'm infiltrating Obsidian's inner circle—at least, I was before you likely blew my cover with that stunt tonight."

"This wasn't a stunt. It was an outright abduction. We need answers about your level of involvement with Obsidian and what you know about what they're planning next."

"I wasn't quite there yet in my operation," Adelman said. "That's why I'd rip you limb from limb right now if I could. Everything I've been working toward over the last year is gone."

"What are they planning?" Hawk asked.

"I already told you that I was in the process of finding that out as I infiltrated the inner circle. But now we won't find out until it's too late."

Hawk resumed circling Adelman as he spoke. "I must say that I'm impressed with your story. It's likely close to the truth, except for the infiltration bit. That's the lie. You've kept everything else close to your real story, and it sounds believable. But I'm not buying it. Unfortunately for your sake, you trained me in the art of deception."

"I'm not trying to deceive you," Adelman said. "I'm merely attempting to explain why I was at Obsidian's event tonight and why this is such a big damn mistake."

"How did you first make contact with Andrei Orlovsky?"

"Who?"

"These games are getting old already. Andrei Orlovsky—how did you meet him?"

"I've heard the name, but I've never made his acquaintance."

"Of course you've heard his name in this underworld you're living in," Hawk said. "Orlovsky is a renowned illegal arms dealer—and your name was at the top of his list of clients."

"What possible reason could I have to work with an arms dealer? You don't suspect that I'm responsible for trying to incite some sort of conflict, do you?"

"I'm not sure what I think at this point," Hawk said. "But I know that you've lost your bearings, Admiral. You were once a great man who loved his country, but now?"

"I'm still that man, Hawk. I'm just disappointed that you can't see it. You're being blinded by your own ambition. And to what end? To prove that you're some super agent after you couldn't make it as a SEAL?"

Hawk narrowed his eyes. "I walked away on my own accord."

"Because you couldn't handle it."

"I couldn't stomach the atrocities I was being ordered to commit as a soldier."

"Those weren't atrocities—that was justice."

Hawk shook his head. "Murdering innocent people is never justice."

"They weren't as innocent as you thought they were. They were—"

"Kids and children and women—they weren't monsters."

Adelman shrugged. "But they would've grown up to be monsters if they weren't already. You should've seen our mission for what it was—a pre-emptive strike."

"You're still the same man now as you were back then," Hawk said. "And that's all the more reason for me not to believe you." He strode toward the door and reached for the knob.

"You're going to regret this, Hawk. One day very soon, you're going to learn that you just set back our efforts to infiltrate Obsidian. And when millions of people are dead after one of their attacks, the blood will be on your hands."

"Worry about your own hands. If you ever find your conscience again, maybe you can commiserate with Lady MacBeth."

Hawk exited the room, slamming the door behind him. He walked down the hall and entered the next door. He eased inside where Alex and Black had been watching the interrogation unfold. Black stroked his chin as he stood and stared at the prisoner, while Alex was hunched over her computer sifting through images captured by Hawk's glasses at the Obsidian event.

"What do you think of that lying bastard?" Hawk asked.

Black shrugged. "He's a bastard all right, but I'm not sure he's lying."

"Oh, come on," Hawk said before exhaling. "You don't really believe Adelman, do you?"

Both men turned and looked at Adelman while Alex remained quiet, engrossed in her work.

"Look at him," Black said, gesturing toward Adelman. "He doesn't appear to be too upset about the accusation. He's just agitated and antsy, ready to get out of here."

"He's acting that way because he knows Obsidian agents will kill him for exposing one of their private meetings like that," Hawk said.

"I don't know," Black said, still studying Adelman. "I'm really unsure. I mean, what if he really is trying to infiltrate Obsidian? He could be a valuable asset for us."

"Even if he was being honest, you think he'd help us?" Hawk asked. "He wouldn't dare want us to get any kind of credit for breaching Obsidian's inner circle and bringing down the organization."

"Let's put egos aside for a moment and weigh what we know," Black said.

"By any measure you use, the scales are tipped against Adelman. He can't prove anything he's saying. Besides, if anyone in the U.S. intelligence community knew about Adelman's operation, Blunt would've heard about it and told us. In fact, he never would've sent us on this mission if Adelman were already in the process of gaining access to Obsidian's leadership. Entertaining the notion that he's telling the truth and is an undercover agent is hardly tenable, much less believable."

Hawk settled into a chair at the table next to Alex. Seconds later, Black followed.

"What do you think, Alex?" Hawk asked.

Her gaze remained fixated on her screen. "I was listening, so I'm just saying this without taking into account Adelman's body language, but I had a difficult time discerning whether his story was true or not. It sounds plausible, but from what you've told me, Adelman seems like an unusual candidate to penetrate an organization like Obsidian."

"They're not a terrorist group," Black said. "So, it's not like Adelman has to live in caves in the desert to gain someone's trust. Obsidian is more like puppet masters. And based on how they operate, it makes sense that they would find value in someone like Adelman."

"You know more than I do about Obsidian," Hawk said. "It all seems strange that Adelman could be doing this without anyone knowing."

"The actual activities of the Phoenix Foundation aren't well known to anyone in Washington, except for maybe the president and General Fortner. So, if the shoe were on the other foot, someone would struggle to believe your story as well."

"He's got a point," Alex said, still focused on her screen.

Hawk sighed. "Maybe you two are right. I just don't like the idea of releasing him yet. There's still more he's not telling us."

Black nodded. "I agree. Even if he is being forthright about his mission, it's not like he can render Obsidian toothless on his own. There needs to be other people attempting to expose them."

"People like us," Hawk said. "My biggest reservation about believing Adelman is that he's exactly the kind of person who would welcome large cash payouts in exchange for helping them. We already know he's stockpiling large sums of money. And while I won't begrudge him of that, he's an admiral in the U.S. Navy. He's not going to be hurting financially when he retires."

Alex abruptly stood, sliding out her chair with the back of her knees. "Guys, where's Adelman?"

Hawk and Black whipped their heads toward the window and peered inside the room.

Adelman's chair was empty, and his bindings were strewn across the table.

"He's gone," Hawk growled.

CHAPTER 13

Washington, D.C.

TWO DAYS LATER, Blunt sat in his office chair, poring over the morning edition of *The Washington Post*. While the security breach may have been contained, there was still plenty of fallout, including the latest news of two other senators announcing they wouldn't run for office again in the upcoming election cycle. Blunt flipped to the sports section for a brief moment of escape. For a few seconds, he pined for the days when he was dead—as far as the rest of the world knew—and living on a sailboat in anonymity.

A knock at his door ended his daydream. He called for the guests to enter the room and watched as Hawk, Alex, and Black all paraded inside. Black and Alex sat down in the two chairs across from Blunt's desk, while Hawk remained standing.

"This is not a meeting I foresaw ever happening," Blunt said. "I preferred to keep you unaware of each other for various reasons. However, circumstances have dictated that we convene to discuss what happened in Hong Kong and how we move forward from here."

Hawk started pacing behind Black and Alex.

"Would you stop that?" Blunt asked. "You're making me nervous, Hawk."

"That makes two of us. I'm always nervous when someone I captured escaped."

He glared at Black, who turned around and returned the stare with one of his own.

"I hope you're not still blaming me," Black said.

"You were the one who insisted on tying up Adelman, not to mention the only one of us who was certain that he was telling the truth about his involvement with Obsidian. I think it's pretty clear now that you were mistaken."

"Just because he escaped doesn't mean he's guilty," Black said. "I've read your file. You've escaped, too, from various captures—and I wouldn't suggest you were guilty in any of those situations."

"I hope you would assume as much since I was never captured simply for interrogation purposes," Hawk said as he narrowed his eyes. "We only wanted to talk with Adelman."

"I doubt he felt that way," Blunt said.

"Well, if he didn't, he was probably wondering

why we didn't use more painful techniques to get him to talk," Hawk said.

"You tied him to a chair," Blunt said. "What else was he supposed to think?"

"Apparently, that didn't seem to matter in the end," Black said.

"Lesson learned," Blunt said. "Now, let's move on from this and formulate a plan for what to do next. With Adelman in the wind and our access to Obsidian being tenuous at best right now, we need a multipronged approach for dealing with all of the crisis facing us at the moment."

"You know my strengths," Black said.

Blunt nodded. "It only took me a few minutes to consider where best to use you, which is in the tracking of Admiral Adelman. We still don't know anything definitively about where he stands, but we need to catch him again and ask him—or at least track his movements and see if we can discern what he's really up to."

"What about us?" Hawk asked.

"For now, I'm going to keep you two together," Blunt said. "That's probably in the best interest of this operation, especially given Alex's ability to trace hackers. I need you to return your focus on identifying who's behind the Undertaker757 handle. Where is he working out of and what his motives are for unleashing such a vicious attack on members of the senate?"

"So, we're just going to ignore Obsidian for the time being?" Hawk asked.

"We don't have much choice in the matter," Blunt said. "I need to move my agents into the positions that give us the best opportunity to succeed. But I have a hunch that these two incidents are all related somehow."

Black nodded. "In my last report, I told you there were rumblings about Obsidian ramping up its operations in an attempt to strike. Who, what, or how are all questions I didn't get answers to yet. But there were rumors that after the all the commodities and services were sold at this latest event, Obsidian leadership was going to invite all of its partners to participate in a big attack and unveil some details about it then. Unfortunately, we never got to that portion of the program thanks to an overly aggressive agent."

Hawk resumed pacing but remained quiet. Blunt held up his hands before speaking in an effort to signal that he'd had enough.

"We're not going to blame one another here," Blunt said. "We're all on the same team, and we need to act like it. I doubt anybody is happy about the way things went down in Hong Kong. We need Adelman to tell us more about his relationship with Andrei Orlovsky as well as get a pulse on what Obsidian is planning. I'm sure everyone thought they were doing what was in the best interest of the overall mission. But we need to be on the same page."

"This is why I prefer working alone," Black said.

"You're not absolved from any wrongdoing in this whole situation," Blunt said. "If you hadn't been so careless in securing Adelman, perhaps we wouldn't even be here having this conversation."

Alex raised her hand. "What do you want us to do with Undertaker757 once we find him?"

"Depends on who he is," Blunt said. "If he's the mastermind, then we'll have the FBI arrest him. But if he can lead us higher up the food chain, we need to proceed with caution. Honestly, I have a difficult time believing that a hacker could be the one ultimately responsible for all this."

Alex chuckled. "You obviously don't know hackers like I do. They're a deviant lot. I wouldn't underestimate any hacker's skill or ideology behind what they're doing. They often misdirect their anger, but they're fervent in what they believe."

"Sounds like a bunch of cult members I once knew," Black said.

"And they're even more dangerous," Alex said. "Just look at what kind of damage they've already been able to do from leaking the private files of all these senators."

"Sounds like everyone has their work cut out for them," Blunt said. "We need to locate Adelman, and we need Undertaker757—and we need them yesterday."

A knock at his door put Blunt's dismissal of his agents on hold. He beckoned the person to enter. Blunt's secretary, Linda, pushed open the door and remained standing there.

"Sir, you might want to turn on the news," she said. "There's something you should see."

Blunt dug into his desk drawer and retrieved his remote control. He turned on the television on the far wall. On the screen, a CNN reporter stood outside the Capitol Building, a ticker across the bottom demarcating that the story was breaking news.

"Utah Senator Warren Philpot, who was the chairman of the senate's foreign relationships committee, has announced his resignation this morning, citing health issues and a desire to spend more time with his family," the dour brunette said.

Blunt slammed his fist onto his desk. "I don't believe that for one minute," he said. "Go get me this hacker so we can put an end to this nonsense."

CHAPTER 14

Washington, D.C.

HAWK AND ALEX ENTERED their office and immediately started to develop a plan to identify and locate the hacker using the Undertaker757 handle. With everything at stake, Hawk reiterated that the plan needed to be foolproof. Any misstep on an operation like this could spell disaster. Alex underscored that point by telling a story about a hacker who the FBI almost caught before he went underground for ten years without even a trace of him online anywhere.

"But they did catch him, right?" Hawk asked.

"Eventually, but not until he made a mistake," Alex said. "The FBI later learned that he had reinvented himself and was the same guy they wanted in a recent spree of cyber-related crimes."

"Have you ever heard of someone operating by the handle of Undertaker757 during your time on the dark web?" Hawk asked.

She shook her head. "That's a popular iteration of a name plenty of hackers have taken, but the numbers at the end are unique."

"Think that could tell us something about who we're looking for?"

"Any hacker who doesn't want to get caught will generate random numbers and tack them on the end of a word he thinks best represents his ideology or mission. But 'undertaker' is a relatively useless moniker for determining anything psychologically about who we're searching for. It might as well be something like Zeus or Bootylicious or DarkAngel. They're all common names used by everybody, but Undertaker is utilized even more so in the hacker world. Everyone there likes to think they can disrupt normal society through their skills in an effort to bring about some sort of justice."

Hawk sighed. "So, digging into those names sounds like a dead end at best."

"I wouldn't completely ignore it," Alex said. "But it's not going to yield any results. Hackers all seem to be cut from the same rebellious cloth."

He gestured toward her with both his hands. "You would be case in point, number one."

Alex snickered. "You know that as well as anyone, don't you?"

"Yes, I do. Now, what do you think is the best

approach for luring Undertaker757 out into the open for a discussion?"

"We're not sure what's driving him, but I'm starting to doubt that it's a financial motivation," Alex said.

"How are you drawing that conclusion?"

"If all these senators are resigning or announcing they won't run in future elections, that seems to be the hacker's end game."

"So, if we're not looking for someone wanting a huge payday, what's the carrot we need to dangle in front of him?" Hawk asked.

"Power, control—or a combination of those two. From what I can tell, the hacker wants to shape the leadership of the U.S. Senate. For what ultimate purpose, I'm not sure, but it's certainly not in the best interest of our country to have one person dictating how those committees are constructed."

"Do you think he might be interested in getting his hands on some of the president's information?" Hawk asked.

Alex's eyebrows shot up. "Now that's a great idea I hadn't considered. Do you think President Young would go along with such a scheme?"

"I think he could be convinced," Hawk said. "I'm thinking we get a benign email that he sent to someone, and we forward it to Undertaker757. Then we wait to see if we get a bite."

"I'm sure he'll be asking questions about how we got his information," Alex said. "That in and of itself would cause me to be suspicious enough."

"Do you think you can pose as if you're part of the North Korean outfit? Maybe you could tell him your facility was temporarily shut down to make upgrade improvements and you needed to develop a new contact name. And then you could say that this is part of your first harvest of new information and have much more where that came from."

"That could work," Alex said. "But I'd rather pose as a hacker who worked at the facility and mention how it was attacked by a covert American operation. I'll first need to seed that idea on some other portion of the dark web so that can be verified, and then I'll have an opportunity to reel him in."

"Sounds like a great plan," Hawk said. "Let's just take a flyer on it. If it doesn't work, then we'll come up with something else."

Alex grimaced. "I don't know. This might be our only shot at snagging him. I'd hate to lose our one connection over a poorly executed operation. Every detail needs to be assessed and reassessed before we launch."

"We don't have time for that. Do you recognize what's happening on Capitol Hill?" Hawk asked.

"Some of our greatest statesmen are being railroaded out of office because of this guy—and he's got a bigger end game in mind. So, let's not worry about getting everything perfect and just throw a line out and hope he takes the bait. My hunch is that he's already feeling confident about what he's been able to do and that he hasn't been caught yet. If he's been able to set this plan in motion without getting arrested, the idea that he could also coopt the president is only going to fuel his desire to seize more control over the government."

"Okay," Alex said. "This makes sense. I can set a trap for him while also working on another way to lure him out in case this one fails. Ultimately, all I need to do is get him talking online in a private manner and keep him there long enough to pinpoint his exact location. Then you can take it from there."

Hawk grinned. "That sounds right up my alley."

"Brains and brawn," Alex said, tapping her temple with her right forefinger and grabbing Hawk's bicep with her left hand.

"Now all that's left to do is convince President Young to give us one of his emails so we can get started," Hawk said.

"Go make that call," she said. "We need to put an end to this as soon as possible."

* * *

HAWK REACHED PRESIDENT YOUNG'S chief of staff through connections with Blunt and put in a request for a meeting. Due to the upcoming G8 summit, Young didn't have time to indulge Hawk with a half-hour conversation, but a five-minute phone call resolved all of Hawk's pressing needs. A few minutes after their talk concluded, an email popped up in Hawk's inbox, forwarded from the president. It was a short note about a tee time Young had scheduled with a senator from an opposing party a couple months prior.

This ought to do the trick. And it's bipartisan, at that.

Later that afternoon, Alex went to work on finding out all of Undertaker757's haunts on the dark web. After two hours of thorough research, she identified what sites he spent most of his time on and devised a way to connect with him. Her next task was to create a profile of someone who had been on the site for a long time. Any suspicious looking correspondence from a newbie to the discussion forum was going to scare him away. If he muted her, it would all be over with. She constructed a plausible profile and volleyed her first question his way.

"Don't you hate politicians these days?" she wrote. The message appeared next to a profile of a busty woman that she found on a royalty-free site. She hated women who flaunted themselves in that manner, but it was almost always guaranteed to attract the attention of most warm-blooded males. Seconds later, a reply popped up, nested neatly beneath her initial inquiry.

"Washington needs to be cleaned out," he wrote. "If only we could vote for other congressional candidates in other states. Ugh."

That statement was followed by a gif of one of the three stooges walking in circles while hitting himself over the head with a frying pan.

Alex smiled and announced to Hawk that she'd made contact.

"Really?" Hawk asked, hustling over to her computer.

"Yeah, and the best part is I didn't even have to use my golden bullet to get him to respond."

Hawk laughed as he looked at the screen. "That's because your avatar makes you look like Pamela Anderson."

"That's not her, is it?" Alex asked, concerned lines spreading across her forehead.

"Oh, you poor thing," Hawk said. "You've never watched an episode of *Baywatch*, have you?"

"I heard it was terrible. Just a bunch of women clad in bikinis bouncing up and down the beach."

"Just a point of clarification—the women wore

one-piece bathing suits, not bikinis."

"But everything else?"

Hawk nodded. "Mostly right. Slow motion pictures of women frolicking on the beach."

"So, I used a picture of Pamela Anderson as my avatar?"

"No, that's not her, but it looks strikingly similar since your girl also has more plastic stuffed in her than a California recycling plant."

Alex snickered. "How long have you been waiting to use that line?"

Hawk shrugged. "I just came up with it. Sounded appropriate given our topic of conversation."

"Wait a minute," Alex said. "It looks like he's writing something else."

The blinking cursor was replaced with a thought bubble. Several seconds later, three sentences appeared.

Are you involved in the rebellion? Do you have any special set of skills? Interested?

"Now that's certainly interesting," Alex said, pointing at the screen. "What do you make of this? Is he recruiting or fishing for information?"

"There's only one way to find out," Hawk said.

Alex looked up at Hawk and grinned. "Bomb's away."

She typed in the address to the secure website where she pasted the email file link that Hawk received from President Young. Then she added an access code along with a little note.

Are these the kind of skills you're looking for?

Alex and Hawk waited for a few moments before a thought bubble appeared, indicating that their target was typing something again. Hawk wondered if he would inspect the document or not.

Nice try, honey, but I'm not about to look at any file like that. You'll need to send me a screenshot of your work if you want to continue our conversation.

Alex sighed. "What now?"

"Send it to him," Hawk said. "And then send him an invitation to talk via another route. Maybe an online game? Can the NSA get access to those?"

She nodded. "Mallory Kauffman. Call her now and get her to help us."

Hawk dialed Mallory's number and gave her the rundown. After she agreed to help, Hawk relayed all the details to her about what they were trying to do.

"Technically, I'm supposed to have a warrant for

this," Mallory said.

"I'm sure we can get one retroactively if we need to use this information to pursue someone in court," Hawk said. "However, I think we may handle this in a different manner."

"As long as J.D. Blunt is a part of this, I'll help," Mallory said.

"Excellent. Stay on the line, and I'll give you all the details."

Hawk pointed at Alex. "You're up."

Alex hammered out a short message and posted a screenshot of the email from President Young. A few seconds later, a terse response came back.

Really? I know an 8yo who can fake something like this.

Alex thought for a moment and then responded.

I have the code here you can look at to prove its authenticity. Nothing fake about it.

"I've got another idea," Alex said. "Let me post this to Wikileaks under a private link, and maybe he'll trust me and go there to visit."

"Do you think he'll still believe you're the one who hacked the White House email server?" Hawk asked.

She shrugged. "Got a better idea right now?"

"All right. Do it," Hawk said.

Alex texted a friend who worked as a volunteer moderator at Wikileaks.

"You know someone who works with Wikileaks?" Hawk asked with mild disbelief.

"I did some dark stuff while working with the CIA," Alex said. "I've got friends everywhere, high places and low ones, too."

"Which category does Wikileaks fall into?"

Alex chuckled. "She's writing me back. Okay, she's agreed to privately post it for me. All she needs is the file."

In less than a minute after forwarding over the email to her friend, Alex received a link. She texted back a quick thank you and then pasted the link into the dialogue box with the Undertaker757 followed by a short note.

Believe me now?

The thought bubble reappeared along with a note a few seconds later.

Nice work. Let's talk.

Alex invited Undertaker757 to chat in the most

secure way possible—an online game. Several lawsuits had been filed by the government in an attempt to gain access to servers from gaming sites to track the conversations of alleged terrorists. Publicly, the ongoing battle in the court system appeared to be tilting in favor of the game makers. However, privately, they gave the NSA and other government surveillance companies unfettered access to search for and track suspicious dialogue in the games. Despite many critics accusing the companies of saving those conversations, the developer insisted that the chats were never meant to be saved and vanished once each game ended. But that was a lie, designed to appease everyone concerned about privacy issues. The NSA shielded the developers from any potential lawsuits because they needed a way to track terrorist communiqués—and it often worked beautifully as most users operated under the assumption that everything they wrote online remained private.

Once she asked him to play the game Fortnite and got his handle—BigKillah29—he agreed, and they began their private conversation.

"Give Mallory all these details," Alex said.

Hawk hustled across the room to his desk and passed the information along to Mallory. She told him that she would call him back once she was able to identify his location.

"Just tell Alex to keep him talking as much as possible to give me time to track him down," Mallory said.

Hawk relayed Mallory's message to Alex and watched her work her magic. In less than a minute, she engaged Undertaker757 in a conversation about the direction of our country and the leadership void among bureaucrats.

"He's eating this up," Alex said.

"Yeah," Hawk said, reading the conversation over her shoulder. "It's like he's intimately acquainted with these people."

"You don't think—nah," Alex said, answering her own question before fully asking it.

"What?" Hawk asked.

"I don't know. I just had a thought, but it's ridiculous."

"No thought it ridiculous when it comes to espionage. Oftentimes, that's why crazy ideas work— nobody would ever believe someone would try it. You know, like utilizing a video game to communicate between terrorist cells."

She sighed. "Well, okay, here it goes. I wonder if this is some kind of inside job."

"Inside in what way?"

"That site in North Korea is a virtual ghost as far as the internet is concerned," Alex said. "They don't even communicate on the dark web."

"So, how did these people get hired?"

"They don't," Alex said as she continued exchanging political banter in the chat session. "I did some online forensics and didn't see a peep or whisper about an outfit like that in North Korea anywhere. I think that was a government operation and someone decided to moonlight their services after a special request came through."

"You think that would be Choe?"

"Yeah, it makes sense. He freaked out when a breach happened because if anyone found out you were there, they'd all be dead somewhere. He complied because he didn't want to get caught. It's the only thing that makes sense about that whole operation."

"What doesn't make sense is how someone knew about what you were doing and then brazenly stole all your equipment."

"I trust Lt. Col. Currant will find the culprit eventually," Alex said.

"Unless he's on Obsidian's payroll as well."

Alex shook her head. "This is a well-oiled machine. There are plenty of conspiracies taking place in order to make that group function to the level that it is. However, I can't see it happening *everywhere* at the highest level. At some point, a whistle blower would come clean and Obsidian would get exposed. They have to be very particular about how they coopt people—and who they coopt—into doing their bidding."

"But you still think Obsidian had someone working for them at the Osan Air Base?"

"I do, but I can't see it being Currant. Just call it a gut feeling, but it doesn't seem likely to me."

"Obsidian at least had someone on that C-17 who tried to kill me."

Alex smiled. "They must not know who you are yet if they sent a child to do a man's job."

"And it better be one hell of a man if he wants to finish the job," Hawk said.

Alex nodded as she pounded away on her phone, responding to the latest barrage of attacks that Undertaker757 unleashed on the American political landscape. The chat continued for ten minutes before Hawk's phone rang.

"I found him," Mallory said. "It wasn't easy because he had IPs pinging all across the globe, so he's no amateur. But I finally identified his exact location based off his online session's originating IP address."

"You know where he is right now?" Hawk asked.

"Yeah, and you're never gonna believe where."

"Try me."

"He's at the Capitol Building in Senator Otto McWilliams's office."

CHAPTER 15

HAWK GRABBED HIS KEYS and hustled outside to bring his car around, while Alex continued to discuss the state of politics with Undertaker757. She eased into the car and groaned as she stared at the screen.

"What is it now?" Hawk asked, easing onto the accelerator.

"We've moved on to the global political climate. How fast can you get to the Capitol? Because I've about had it with this moron."

"I'll let you tell him that to his face when we get there—ten, maybe fifteen, minutes tops."

Hawk weaved in and out of traffic in an attempt to shave a couple minutes off his ETA. But in Washington, such efforts usually resulted in dismal failure. He sat at a traffic light for two minutes, and his lane didn't move.

"Come on," Hawk said aloud, hitting steering wheel in frustration.

"We'd probably be better off taking the metro if I knew my connection would hold up underground," Alex said.

He sighed. "This mission has taken quite a turn."

"Fontenot immediately dismissed any possibility that McWilliams was involved. Obviously he doesn't know one of his best friends as well as he says he does."

"Are we certain McWilliams is actually the one pulling the trigger on this thing?"

Alex shrugged. "I guess we'll find out when we get there as long as I can keep him talking online."

"What's he saying now?" Hawk asked as he eased onto the brake at a traffic light.

"He's moved on to how evil the G8 is. Whoever this guy is, no current iteration of government pleases him. He won't be satisfied unless he's the one running the show."

"Maybe it is McWilliams then," Hawk said, jamming his foot onto the gas as the light turned green. "I've heard his name bandied about as a potential rival to President Young in the next election."

Alex cocked her head and looked at Hawk. "But would he really be doing something like this, sitting in his office connecting with people on the dark web and griping about the state of affairs in the world? It just seems—I don't know, nutty."

As they pulled into an underground garage lot near the Capitol Building, Alex groaned.

"What is it now?" Hawk asked.

"No, no, no, no," she said, tapping on her phone's keyboard screen. "Stay with me."

"Is he still there?"

"He said he has to go and just logged off."

Hawk hit the brakes, and they came to a stop in one of the parking spots.

"We have to move quickly," Alex said.

They darted out of the car and broke into a dead sprint toward the famed congressional building. Weaving in and out of meandering tourists and reckless Segway drivers zipping along the sidewalk, Hawk and Alex made it to the steps and raced toward the door. They hustled through security and sprinted toward McWilians's office, the location which Alex found on her phone while they were running.

Once they reached his offices, they rushed inside and found an elderly woman named Clara Bartenfield, according to the nameplate, positioned on the front of her desk. She was leaning back in her chair and nursing a cup of tea. Alex began peppering Clara with questions while she was still in the middle of sipping her drink.

"Is Senator McWilliams still here?" Alex asked.

"Has he already gone for the day? Are there any other staffers around?"

Hawk watched Alex's countenance transform from hope to despair in an instant.

"I'm afraid I'm the only one here at the moment," she said.

Hawk was still trying to process the meaning of Clara's answer as he studied her.

If she's the only one here, could she be the one chatting on the dark web?

It was certainly a conclusion that he didn't expect to make, but he couldn't rule anything out given all the other oddities that had occurred since he and Alex were assigned to this mission. The idea that the mild-mannered woman in front of him was directing a takeover of the U.S. political scene with the help of North Korean hackers seemed highly unlikely—if not improbable. But he wasn't willing to rule anyone out after all he'd just witnessed. Alex, however, wasn't about to concede that she could've been the culprit.

"I mean is there *anyone* here right now?" Alex repeated. "A custodian, a low-level staffer, an intern—anyone?"

She shook her head resolutely. "Just me."

"What about a few minutes ago? Was anyone else in this office within the past five minutes?" Alex asked.

"Other than Senator McWilliams?" Clara asked.

"*Anyone*," Hawk said.

"Well, the senator was on a phone call for about an hour with his campaign manager back home in Florida. And then he left."

"Are you absolutely sure?" Hawk asked.

"It's my job to know where everyone is and what they're doing," Clara said. "I might look old to you, but I sure as hell can manage an office."

"So, the senator was the only one here?" Alex pressed again.

Clara put her index finger up in the air. "No, wait a minute. There was another worker here. His name is Derek Thurston. I don't really know him that well because he's fairly new, and I'm not sure what it is that he does. But he comes and goes as he pleases. However, he left maybe fifteen minutes ago. He's like a ghost most days."

"Is there anything you know about him?" Alex asked.

"Other than the fact that he's a jerk?" she asked.

Alex nodded.

"Not much to know, really," Clara said. "He was a private first class in the U.S. Army but couldn't ascend above that rank. I think he was a disappointment to his parents, especially his father who eventually rose through the army's ranks to become a four-star general. And here's little ole Derek, who can't hold his temper resulting in him essentially earning an early exit from the military. Major disappointment would be more like it."

"And you say you don't know much about him," Alex said.

"Well, I read his file and spoke with one of the former FBI agents who profiled him for us," Clara said. "And honestly, yes, I don't know much about him in comparison to everyone else. I don't know his girlfriend's name or his favorite baseball team or if he prefers blue pens or black pens or—"

"Where do you people park?" Hawk asked, his patience with Clara waning.

Clara pointed behind her. "There's an official parking lot on the east side of the building."

"Do you know what kind of car he drives?" Alex asked.

"A red Dodge Charger," Clara answered before launching into a tedious story about the history of her first parking space at the Capitol Building.

"I don't mean to be rude, but we need to get going," Hawk said. "Thank you for your time and the information."

Hawk and Alex dashed out the door and took off running down the hallway.

"Think you can get a license plate for Derek Thurston?" Hawk asked.

"I'm already on it," Alex said as she glanced down at her phone. Seconds later, she was speaking with Linda at the Phoenix Foundation about looking up Thurston's registration and home address. After she hung up, they increased their pace.

"Did you bring your computer along with you?" Hawk asked.

"Always. I'll be able to track him on traffic cams as we go."

"We may not have to," Hawk said as they arrived near the employee lot.

"That's him," Alex said, pointing at his car.

They sprinted toward him just as he got into his Charger. He casually started the car until he noticed Hawk and Alex rushing toward him. Stomping on the gas, his tires barked as he whipped out of his space and toward the exit. Hawk and Alex backed away.

"Glad I got his plates," Alex said.

"Let's hustle," Hawk said.

The garage they had parked in was just across the street. Sprinting to Hawk's car, they jumped inside and took off.

Hawk began his pursuit by choosing a direct route to Thurston's apartment while Alex searched for him on her computer using closed circuit feeds.

"Got him," she announced after a couple minutes. "And we need to go west. Looks like he's headed somewhere in Virginia."

Hawk followed Alex's directions as they tried to track Thurston through stop-and-go rush hour traffic. After an hour of following his path, they rolled up behind him. Hawk flashed his lights in an effort to get Thurston to stop.

"You think he's going to just pull over?" Alex asked as she put away her computer.

"It was worth a shot."

"He's not going to do us any favors."

The traffic light in front of them turned red and both cars, which were at the front of the line, slowed down. However, just as the vehicles in the cross lanes started to move, Thurston accelerated forward. He weaved around a truck and a van before navigating through the intersection without causing an accident.

Hawk cursed as he slammed his fist on the steering wheel.

"Wait a minute," Alex said. "Don't get too upset just yet. We can still catch him."

"How?"

"There's not much on this road except for a rock quarry up ahead on the right and a few hobby farms."

The light turned green, and Hawk tore off after Thurston.

"Right there," Alex said, tapping at her window. "You can still see the dust. He turned into the quarry."

Hawk jerked the car to the right and drove into the quarry, which appeared to be devoid of any employees.

"This ought to be fun," Hawk said as he scanned the area for any signs of Thurston's Charger.

"Look," Alex said, pointing toward the far west corner of the property. "I think I see him over there. He's on foot."

Hawk parked his car and eased out. His door was still open when a couple bullets whizzed in his direction.

"Stay here and stay down," Hawk said.

He checked his gun and then crept in the opposite direction. Sneaking around a pile of rocks, he tried to get into a better position to see Thurston. But he had abandoned his previous location and was on the move.

Hawk swiveled around to see if Thurston was behind him. From what Hawk could see, Thurston was not nearby. Fifty meters away, a conveyor belt hummed as it started operating. Large chunks of rocks chugged upward toward a grinder, distracting Hawk for a second. Another shot pinged off the nearby rocks and sent Hawk scrambling to get down.

Crawling on his belly, Hawk regained his composure and sought out the best spot to locate Thurston. Twenty meters behind Hawk was another grinder with a ladder. He climbed to the top and peered out over the yard for Thurston. He was huddled near a pile of rocks, contemplating his next move.

Gotcha.

Hawk stole around the back of the quarry and waited for the right moment to press in and capture Thurston. After a minute, Thurston dug his phone out of his pocket while keeping his head on a swivel. He let his defenses down for a moment to dial a number, which is when Hawk raced toward his target.

Thurston looked up just in time to get pistol whipped in the forehead. He folded like a cheap tent, collapsing to the ground in a heap.

CHAPTER 16

Washington, D.C.

THE PHOENIX FOUNDATION officially owned just one building. However, Blunt set up a CIA-sanctioned shell company to facilitate the purchase of a pair of underground facilities for staging and interrogation purposes. Hawk and Alex sped toward the site located just off the Potomac. Upon arriving, Hawk opened the trunk and pulled out a groggy and disoriented Derek Thurston.

With Hawk's help, Thurston stumbled inside and fell into a chair in the middle of a small interview room. The room had a two-way mirror on the far wall and a small desk in the center with a chair on each side.

"What's going on here?" Thurston asked.

Hawk used some parachute cord to bind Thurston's wrists behind his back and to the chair.

"Do you really need to ask that question?" Hawk replied. "You were the one who led us to a rock quarry and then opened fire. I think you know good and well what's going on."

Thurston shook his head emphatically, writhing against the bindings, which Hawk had just finished securing.

"I swear. I don't know anything. Who are you? And why are you doing this to me?"

Alex sauntered into the room and stooped down to get eye level with the captive. "Perhaps we can play Fortnite together sometime again soon, Mr. Undertaker757."

Thurston set his jaw. "I knew that was a trap. I should've never written you back."

"Avatars with low-cut shirts and big busts," Alex said. "They're absolutely irresistible, aren't they?"

Thurston sneered at Alex and then looked away.

"You're going to have to face the music," Hawk said. "We know you were the one behind all this."

"It wasn't me. I swear," Thurston said.

Hawk fished Thurston's phone out of his pocket and depressed his thumb to the security button. When the home screen vanished, Hawk handed the phone to Alex. She swiped over to the video game and opened it to inspect the avatar.

"If it's BigKillah29, you're in trouble," she said before studying the screen for a few seconds. "Well, what do you know? Your handle is BigKillah29. Now how did I know that if you weren't involved in anything?"

Thurston shifted in his seat and then looked down at his feet.

"We didn't put a gag on you," Hawk said. "You're expected to answer these questions one way or another. Now, I'll give you a pass on this first once since we already know the answer. But you better be more forthcoming in the future. Are we clear?"

Thurston nodded. His army physique hadn't completely disappeared, but he had put on a few pounds around his waist since leaving the military. However, Hawk wondered if his prisoner ever spent any time in combat and instead had spent all his time in the field behind a computer screen.

"Let's start at the top," Hawk said. "Tell us about how Obsidian first contacted you."

"Ob—what? I definitely don't know what you're talking about," Thurston said.

"Obsidian, the organization you're working for," Hawk said.

Thurston furrowed his brow. "I'm not working for anybody by that name. I just—"

"You've been warned about the consequences of stonewalling us, so you might want to reconsider your answer before I move you to a different room where we ask questions in a far less polite manner."

"Look, I just had some guy ask me if I wanted to make some extra cash," Thurston explained. "I'm the low man on the totem pole in Senator McWilliams's office, and it's expensive to live in Washington. So, I agreed to help him out. But when I heard what he wanted, I told him no."

"There's more, isn't there?"

Thurston nodded. "After I declined the offer, I got a call from my girlfriend in Seattle. She was planning on joining me at the end of the month after she fished up grad school, but those plans were put on hold when she was kidnapped."

"Did you report her missing?" Hawk asked.

"They told me if I said anything that they would kill her."

"And this story hasn't made the news yet?" Alex asked.

"They had her withdraw from her classes and then call in to announce that she was quitting her job. She was a pretty private person and didn't have any roommates, so all I can figure is that with all her social connections severed, nobody's realized she's missing yet. But it's only been two weeks since this all began."

"Did they say when they were going to release her?" Hawk asked.

"When they were satisfied that they had all the information they needed, they said they would release her. I'm still gathering info, but I only send it when they ask."

"I need the email address of the person you're working with," Alex said, pulling out a piece of paper and a pen from her computer bag.

"I—I don't know if that's such a good idea," Thurston said.

"If you want to see her alive, I suggest you trust us," Hawk said.

"I don't even know who you guys you are or who you work for. You threw me in the back of your trunk and who knows where we are. So pardon me if I'm running a little low in the trust department these days."

"I understand," Hawk said. "All I can tell you is that we're special agents Miller and Roman and we work for the government. Is that enough for you?"

"No, it's not. I need to see identification."

Hawk shrugged. "Sorry, we don't carry any. For most of our operations, it's best that way."

"Then this is all bullshit," Thurston said. "For all I know, you're with the same people who are strong arming me into doing their dirty work and you just want to see if I'll crack."

"When was the last time you heard from your contact?" Alex asked.

"Three days ago. Why?"

"Because they're done with you," Alex said. "And if we were working with them, we would've killed you already and not gone through painstaking lengths to assure your safety. Besides, what do you have to lose?"

"My girlfriend, for starters."

"We'll bring all our resources to bear in order to get her back for you," Hawk said. "We'll call in favors and get the best people on the job to get her back safely. That's what I can promise you if you're willing to work with us."

"Fine," Thurston said. "I'll help. But I don't know what good it's going to do."

Hawk pulled out his knife and sliced through the cord around Thurston's hands.

"Write down everything," Alex said. "All the contacts, all the protocols. And I'll need the email address and password you use to communicate with them. We'll likely need to do this from whatever computer you normally use when contacting them."

Thurston nodded and started writing.

Hawk tugged on Alex's sleeve, gesturing for her to join him in the corner.

"You think you can make this work?" Hawk asked in a whisper.

"I'll see what I can do, but there are no guarantees. We're still feeling out just how ruthless these people are and what they're fully capable of doing."

"We already know that they're incredibly dangerous."

Alex nodded. "I think there are plenty of layers to the organization. And this isn't going to be a simple operation by any stretch of the imagination."

CHAPTER 17

HAWK AND ALEX DROVE Thurston to his apartment and got to work. Alex doctored some images to make it appear as though several prominent senators were in compromising situations with women other than their wives. When she was finished, Thurston let out a long whistle.

"If I didn't know any better, I'd think that was real," he said.

"That's the point," Alex said. "However, I'm only trying to pique their interest enough so they open the image. The subject line and message will be what sells this. They won't know what's in the images until they click."

"The handler told me that I'm only to respond to his emails, not initiate anything," Thurston said.

"I think we can get around that," Alex said with a wink.

She returned her focus to the computer and started to hammer away on the keyboard. A half hour later, she stood and announced that she was finished, triumphantly raising her hands in the air.

"You're ready to send it?" Hawk asked.

She nodded. "Read this and tell me what you think."

Hawk scanned the email, which had a tantalizing subject line: "If you thought what I sent you before was . . ." He chuckled as he looked at the note.

"You should work for one of those click bait companies, Alex. This is excellent. I have to know what's inside here."

"Maybe one day," she said. "Honestly, I would like to get revenge on all those companies who post click bait headlines and stuff them into endless slideshows. I bet I've wasted two months of my life scrolling through something that could've been said in one paragraph."

Thurston started laughing, the first moment of shared levity since he was corralled by Hawk and Alex.

"Why don't you compile all these pictures into a slideshow?" Thurston said.

Alex wagged her finger at Thurston. "Because we want to punish these people in far more excruciating ways. And we don't want to make them so mad that they don't return your girlfriend."

Thurston sighed as the smile vanished from his face.

"Yeah, I know Maya would appreciate that."

"That's her name?" Alex asked. "Maya?"

"Yes, Maya Walker. She's an amazing woman and was about to get her masters in public health from the University of Washington. She had a fellowship already lined up here, so I don't know what's going to happen now."

Hawk caught a sideways glance from Alex and understood her look.

"Why don't we have a drink over in the living room so Alex can finish up," Hawk suggested. "Do you have any beer or bourbon?"

"The pantry is fully stocked with liquor, and there's beer in the fridge."

"Excellent," Hawk said. "What do you want?"

"Surprise me," Thurston said.

Hawk returned to the living room with a pair of tumblers filled halfway with bourbon. They continued to shoot the breeze while Alex sent off her email.

Ten minutes later, she pumped her fist and stood to celebrate.

"They took the bait," she said.

Hawk and Thurston hustled over to her to glean more details.

"Did they write back?" Thurston asked.

"Not yet," Alex said just before a ping designated a new message had just arrived in her inbox.

"Ask and ye shall receive," Thurston said.

Alex clicked on the message and read it aloud: "Thanks for your generous offer, but I believe I warned you not to initiate any contact with us. We will contact you."

"Didn't he read what you wrote?" Thurston asked.

Alex shrugged. "I explained why I was breaking protocol, that I just couldn't contain my excitement over these salacious images."

Thurston sighed. "I hope this doesn't come back on Maya."

"Well, if it does, I apologize," Alex said. "However, he opened the pictures, which means the code I embedded will soon send me details of their exact location based off the IP address."

"But you can spoof an IP address," Thurston said.

Hawk nodded. "We know that all too well. And apparently, you're pretty good at it."

"You can fool outside servers, but your own computer knows where it is—and that's the information I'm after."

They all read and re-read the message before Alex's phone pinged with a text message. She smiled as she read it.

"This is my report coming back to me," she said

as she placed her phone down on the desk. She copied the IP address from her phone into a special CIA website on Thurston's laptop.

"Bingo," she said, pointing at the screen.

A map appeared where a blinking red dot denoted the exact location along with an address.

"How did you do that?" Thurston asked.

"A good magician never tells her secrets," Alex said as she hurriedly wrote down the information on a sheet of paper.

She then entered the address and started scouring the internet for more information about the place where Maya Walker was being held. Her mouth fell agape, and she peered more closely at a list rendered by her search.

"Hawk, you're not gonna believe this."

"Try me," Hawk said.

"This property belongs to a company owned by Mike Paxton."

"The Mike Paxton?" Hawk asked in disbelief.

She nodded. "Yes, the former senator Mike Paxton."

CHAPTER 18

Wintergreen, Virginia

THE NEXT MORNING, Alex drove Hawk and Thurston in the team's surveillance van to Wintergreen Resort. Hawk expressed his reservations about letting Thurston tag along, but Alex made the case that his presence might turn out to be valuable should they catch Mike Paxton.

Paxton was a former Virginia senator who had his heart set on winning the White House. However, a couple of illegal campaign finance charges scuttled those hopes and, with it, all the influence he'd amassed in Washington after serving three terms. His personal financial situation didn't suffer as he landed in the resort community of Wintergreen, but he pined away about losing his ability to steer policy and sway politicians to join in on certain legislation.

In his mid-fifties, Paxton was still in good shape and often posted photos of himself training for and running in Iron Man races. Alex had noted on more than one occasion that she hoped Hawk was still that fit when he reached Paxton's age.

The morning operation was simple: capture Paxton and make him talk. Hawk and Alex wanted to get Paxton to order Maya Walker's release initially before gleaning other pertinent information to begin a systematic takedown of Obsidian. But Alex cautioned that this was going to take a while and the Phoenix team couldn't get ahead of itself.

"One step, then another," Alex had said.

Hawk sighed. He preferred to dive in headlong and hope to emerge victorious. It was an approach that worked so well for him, but Alex was often the voice of descent, countering that there was wisdom in proceeding with caution when attacking a group as networked as Obsidian.

Hawk caught Alex sneaking a peek on him as he finished suiting up with his body armor.

"You look like you're ready for an all-out war with Paxton," Alex said.

"Don't act like you haven't seen his posts on Instagram," Hawk said. "He might be older than me, but you know he's built like a gladiator. I can't leave anything to chance."

She smiled. "I'm glad you're thinking that way, because I'm going to be very upset if something happens to you on account of your poor preparation."

Hawk glared at her. "You know I'm always prepared."

"That's why you always come home—and you always *better* come home because God help you if you don't."

"Just relax, Alex," he said. "I'm ready for whatever he throws at me."

Alex slowed to a stop a few hundred meters away from the gated driveway leading up to Paxton's home. A staggered brick fence demarcated the boundary along with a plethora of pine trees that soared above the property. Situated on a ridge, the sprawling two-story brick home cast a dark shadow over the front yard as the sun peeked just above the mountains on the eastern side of the lake.

"Go get him," Alex said.

Hawk opened the door and saluted her before crouching low and hustling across the road. He made his way toward Paxton's house and climbed over the fence once he reached the edge. Moving toward the house, Hawk used the trees for cover until he was standing a few feet away from a side entrance.

The garage door jerked upward, catching Hawk off guard. He jumped and hustled behind Paxton's bass boat sitting on an unhitched trailer. When Hawk turned his attention back toward the garage, he saw

Paxton—and Paxton saw Hawk.

Hawk rushed toward him, but Paxton scrambled inside and locked the door. Backing away, Hawk sought cover—and it was a good thing he did as Paxton returned armed with a gun.

Paxton squeezed off a couple rounds, sending Hawk diving behind the boat again.

"I don't know what you want, but I'm warning you to leave me alone," Paxton yelled. "I will kill you if I get the opportunity—and I can promise you that nobody is going to know about it. You'll disappear and your relatives will never know what happened to you. That's a promise I will keep."

Hawk wasn't deterred by the warning. Instead, he sought a new route to the house to capture Paxton. After a few minutes, Paxton shut the garage door and went back inside.

"How's it going out there?" Alex asked. "I heard gun shots, but I can tell you're still alive and kicking."

"Alive? Yes. Kicking? Not so much."

"Did you get injured?" Alex asked frantically.

"No, I'm fine, but this isn't going to be so simple. It's obvious that he's not real keen on the idea of being forced to go somewhere against his will."

"Who ever is?" Alex fired back.

"Good point," Hawk said. "In the meantime, I need to figure out a way to flush him out."

"So you don't think the 'enter with guns blazing' approach is going to work best in this situation?"

"That's a big negative," Hawk said.

"Why don't you sneak inside?" she asked.

"Maybe I don't have to," he said. "Someone just walked out the back door."

Paxton lumbered down the steps, his gun stuffed into his pants. He scanned the area. Satisfied that it was clear, he grabbed his putter and a handful of golf balls out of his bag sitting at the foot of the steps. Then he walked over to the putting green installed in his back yard and began to practice.

Hawk eased around the side and tried to determine the best way to approach Paxton. Deciding to wait until he had his back turned, Hawk edged closer whenever he could tell Paxton's attention was focused elsewhere. After a few minutes, Hawk was close enough that he could estimate making it to the green before Paxton had time to turn around and see what was coming.

As soon as Paxton looked down to address his putt, Hawk took off running toward his target. However, before he could get there, Paxton dropped his putter and darted through the bushes. He weaved left and right before dashing down an embankment dotted with pine trees.

"What's your status, Hawk?" Alex asked.

"The target is on the run," Hawk said.

"Anything we can do to help?"

"Negative. He's racing along the ridge and is going away from you."

"Roger that. Keep us apprised of your situation."

With Paxton still in Hawk's sites, he began to wonder how the man had so much stamina. Hawk couldn't tell where Paxton was ultimately headed or if he was simply taking Hawk on a wild goose chase. Either way, Paxton's familiarity with the terrain gave him a significant advantage in the chase. Hawk needed to use his wits if he was going to catch Paxton and wrangle him to the ground.

Up ahead, Paxton darted behind a boulder and then vanished. Hawk combed the area and didn't see any signs of the former senator.

"Where the hell did he go?" Hawk asked.

"Need some help?" Alex asked over the coms.

"I'd love some," Hawk said.

"I'm picking up a heat signature about thirty meters to your right. I wish I could do better and tell you what he's doing, but the tree canopy provides too much cover for the satellite."

"This should be good enough," Hawk said.

He moved toward the location Alex gave him, utilizing the trees again for cover. After a minute, he sought more specific direction.

"Am I close?" he asked

"There's a big boulder about five meters away," she said. "He's behind that."

Hawk crept around the corner and was nearly bowled over. Diving to the ground, he rolled aside to avoid absorbing a head-on collision. When he gathered himself, he looked over to see a large deer prancing off through the forest.

"Alex, that was a buck," Hawk said. "I know you know the difference between those two heat sigs."

"He must've been lying down," she said. "I thought maybe it was Paxton."

"Then we lost him?" Hawk asked.

"No, wait. I see something else moving along the ridge."

Hawk looked up and peered into the distance and saw the back of Paxton hustling along a trail. "I see him now."

He broke into a dead sprint, gaining on Paxton but at a slower than preferable rate. Once Paxton realized he was still being pursued, he kept looking over his shoulder to see how close Hawk was. While Paxton was glancing back to check on his lead, he tripped and tumbled, skidding along the ground.

Hawk dug deeper and increased his speed yet again. However, Paxton scrambled behind a tree and sat there.

"You're almost there," Alex said.

"I know where he's at," Hawk said. "If he starts to move, let me know."

Hawk eased to within ten meters of the tree providing a marginal amount of cover for Paxton.

"Senator Paxton, we need to talk," Hawk said.

Silence.

"I know you're back there," Hawk said. "Our surveillance cameras are following you. There's no way for you to escape."

"Who are you?" Paxton asked.

"I'm just a friend, someone who needs some information from you. There's a girl's life in danger, and I think you might be able to help save her."

Paxton laughed. "That's not why you're really here, is it? Who sent you?"

"Just come out and let's talk," Hawk said. "I'm putting my weapon down now. You can peek around the corner and see. I'm not here to harm you. I just want to have a little conversation."

"Then why did you come dressed like that?"

"I was a Boy Scout," Hawk said. "I'm always prepared for the worst, but I—"

"Plan for the best, yada, yada, yada. I know, I know. It's a boring way to live."

"At the moment, it's keeping me alive," Hawk said. "And I happen to think that's a good thing."

"In that case, you really don't know what you're getting yourself into, do you?"

"Senator Paxton, I haven't even told you why I'm really here. But I guess I don't have to tell you, do I?"

"I never wanted them to take that girl, but you just don't understand how they work."

"How who works?" Hawk asked.

"Them, the real enemy, the people you should be pursuing instead of me."

"That's what I'm trying to do, but I need your help. Call them and tell them to let her go."

"You're on a fool's errand. You're going to die if you don't stop what you're doing."

"That's my call, not yours."

"You'll be like me, forever haunted, forever chased. I can't even find true peace up here on this beautiful mountainside."

"Your peace shouldn't be dictated by your circumstances," Hawk said. "You can find peace anywhere, even in the midst of a violent storm."

"This isn't a storm I'm in," Paxton said. "This is hell, the real live version of it. And there's only one way to stop it."

Hawk took a deep breath and closed his eyes. He could sense he was losing Paxton but wasn't about to give up.

"Don't do it," Hawk said. "There are people who

love you and people who can protect you from Obsidian."

"No, nobody can protect you from Obsidian. They're everywhere, and they will continue to wrap their tentacles around every part of your life until there's nothing left to do but succumb to your fate. It's what they do to each person they involve in their schemes—and it's what they're about to do to the entire world."

"What kind of scheme are you talking about?" Hawk asked.

"The kind that you can't stop."

"Senator Paxton, you can still help us. I'll fight against them even if it's the last thing I do."

Paxton chuckled before answering. "It most certainly will be the last thing you do. And this is the last thing I will say."

"No!" Hawk screamed.

But it was too late. The gunshot echoed through the forest as Hawk watched Paxton's body slide along the tree before hitting the ground with a thud.

"Hawk? What's your status?" Alex asked.

"I'm fine, but Paxton isn't. Self-inflicted gunshot to the head."

Hawk walked over to inspect the body. Something on Paxton's wrist caught Hawk's eye. Kneeling down to inspect the marking closer, he recognized it as it came into full view.

"Paxton was bought and paid for," Hawk said. "He had an Obsidian tattoo on his wrist."

"Hustle back," Alex said. "With Paxton out of the picture, we're going to have to storm the facility. There's a team outside right now just waiting on the word."

"Send them in," Hawk said. "I'll meet you back at the van shortly."

* * *

ALEX TYPED IN a few commands on her computer screen, which quickly transformed into a portal showing four windows with different live body armor video feeds. Thurston stuck his head next to hers in an effort to catch a glimpse.

"I'm not sure it's a good idea for you to watch this," Alex said. "You might see something you'll later regret. And I can promise you that there are some things you just can't un-see, images that will stick with you for the rest of your life when you close your eyes at night."

"I have to watch this," Thurston said. "I have to know if Maya is okay or not."

"You might rather just hear a report first before you see any video of what's happening. If it's ugly—"

"Just give the command. I'm going to watch."

Alex shrugged, resisting the urge to continue her

pleas. Thurston would see the image—for better or worse—in a matter of moments. She hoped it wouldn't be the latter.

"Move in," Alex said into her microphone, giving the command to the SWAT team positioned outside the Seattle warehouse.

She watched as the team used a battering ram to blast through the door. Agents swarmed inside the facility, which was dark. Their infrared video feeds captured the various rooms. Most were used as storage, filled with broken chairs and desks, symbolic of the dashed dreams once held by the company that occupied the building.

"What is all that?" Thurston asked.

"The team is just clearing each room," Alex said. "We know someone was operating out of this place, but no guarantees that she's being held captive here as well."

Just over a minute into the operation, one of the agents stopped and cursed under his breath.

"What is it, Wilder?" the team leader asked.

"You need to come see this," the agent responded.

The body cam on Wilder was directed at the far wall.

"What's in there?" Thurston asked as he leaned over Alex's shoulder.

"I don't know," she said, trying once more to dissuade him from looking. "Maybe you don't want to see this."

Thurston gasped as the image came into view.

Maya Walker was dead in the corner—and looked like she'd been that way for at least several days.

CHAPTER 19

Washington, D.C.

THE NEXT MORNING, Blunt watched as Hawk and Alex trudged into his office and slumped into the chairs across from him. Blunt folded up his copy of the morning newspaper and placed it on the corner of his desk. Leaning back in his chair, he interlocked his fingers behind his head and took a deep breath.

"Cheer up, you two," Blunt said. "If I didn't know any better, I would've thought your spouses died."

"Yesterday was rough," Hawk said as he rested his forehead on his right hand.

"The Undertaker757 turned out to be a dead end in more ways than one," Alex added. "Hearing him wail in agony as he realized his girlfriend was dead was my least favorite part of yesterday."

"And that only just behind watching Senator Paxton take his own life in the woods," Hawk added.

"So it was a rough day at the office," Blunt said. "What you've been able to accomplish so far has been greeted warmly by many members of congress."

Hawk huffed a soft laugh through his nose. "Of course it has," he said. "We've kept some of their skeletons in the closet—for now. Why wouldn't they be happy?"

"Don't be so cynical, Hawk," Blunt said. "Everyone hides skeletons. It's just that most people don't have some nefarious group combing through their garbage to find a shred of damning evidence that will result in public embarrassment and possibly even loss of a job."

"But Obsidian is still out there, pulling the strings with whoever they can coerce into doing their bidding," Alex said. "And that's something we're not happy about."

"Neither am I, but we have to celebrate the wins when we can," Blunt said.

"I don't consider yesterday a win by any stretch of the imagination," Hawk said.

Blunt nodded. "Perhaps, but you've managed to contain a situation that had this town teetering on the edge of chaos."

"I'm not sure I feel like we've done a good thing then," Hawk said.

"Scandals are relative," Blunt said, "especially

when the media is the one involved in trying to air everyone's dirty laundry to benefit the party of their constituents' choice."

"Still," Alex said, "we feel like we're fighting an uphill battle. We're no closer to making a dent in Obsidian than we were a week ago."

Linda knocked on the door, interrupting their meeting.

"What is it, Linda?" Blunt asked.

"Titus Black is on line two for you, sir," she said. "He said it's urgent." She spun around and returned to her desk.

"This ought to be interesting," Blunt said before selecting the button and placing the call on speaker phone.

"Good morning, Black," Blunt said. "I've got Hawk and Alex in the room with me. What do you have for us?"

"Something that's going to make your day," Black said.

"You have news on Admiral Adelman?" Blunt asked.

"Sure do. Tracked him to the South Pacific in Vanuatu, a place with no U.S. extradition."

Hawk grinned. "Good thing we're not trying to extradite him then, isn't it?"

"Do you want the honors?" Blunt asked.

"No," Black said. "Let Hawk and Alex go. I heard they never really got the honeymoon they always wanted. Besides, I need to take some time off and rest. Tracking him down was quite a chore."

"Consider it done," Blunt said before ending the call. "Well, you two, it looks like you're headed to the South Pacific."

CHAPTER 20

Port Vila, Vanuatu

TWO DAYS LATER, Hawk and Alex strolled onto the docks used primarily for Vanuatu's private sailing vessels. The flight from the day before was long, and they had decided to get a good night of sleep before attempting to apprehend Admiral Adelman. A light breeze and the smell of salt water in the South Pacific made Hawk pine for a real vacation with Alex, one where they could truly unwind. But he knew such longing would only result in temporary satisfaction.

Hawk looked at Alex and took her hand in his. She glanced up at him and smiled.

"Seems kind of strange that we're on an operation right now, enjoying a nice walk near the shore in such a beautiful place," she said. "We even have a private jet at our beck and call."

"This is nice," Hawk said. "But I think we both know how quickly we'd get tired of this."

She nodded knowingly. "At least we can share a moment like this while working. Not many people can say that."

"Not many people can say a lot of things about the life we lead."

Hawk approached one of the attendants and inquired about locating a particular vessel.

"Do you know if the boat has been here for a few days?" the man asked.

Hawk nodded.

"Go talk to someone in the office," the man said. "We have a register that must be signed by everyone who docks here. But that information doesn't come cheap. We're very serious about the privacy of our guests."

The man winked and smiled before resuming his task.

"Got any cash?" Alex asked after they turned away.

"Think a Benjamin will do the trick?" Hawk replied.

She shrugged. "Let's go find out."

They walked over to the office and entered. A brass bell clanked against the glass door as it fell shut. A balding portly gentleman with a thick Polynesian accent greeted them as he walked from behind the counter.

"Welcome to Vanuatu," he said. "What can I help you with today?"

Hawk scanned the area to make sure no one was within earshot as he and Alex approached the man.

"We're looking for a boat," Hawk said.

The man chuckled as he walked back behind the counter. "You've come to the right place. We have many boats for sale."

Hawk shook his head. "I mean, we're looking for a specific one that's docked here at the moment."

The man shrugged. "Sorry, but I cannot help you. That information is private. However, you are free to wander the docks on your own."

Hawk pulled out the hundred dollar bill and slid it across the counter.

"We're kind of short on time and were hoping you might give us a better idea of where we might be able to find a catamaran named *Lesson Learned*."

The man stroked his chin for a few seconds before divulging the information.

"Now, don't let anyone know you heard it from me," he said with a smile.

"Don't worry," Hawk said. "I'll keep this between us."

"Good luck," the man said as he waved.

Hawk and Alex exited the office and headed toward the boat Black linked Adelman to.

Lesson Learned was a 45-foot catamaran, dwarfed in the harbor by larger luxury yachts. Tucked away near a portion of the dock reserved for smaller ships, Adelman was hosing down the deck when he looked up and made eye contact with Hawk and Alex. Trapped for making an escape on land, he sought a different route. The boat next to him had a raft with an outboard motor attached that was tied up. Adelman loosened the ropes and then yanked the starter. The engine sputtered to life.

Hawk and Alex both sprinted toward the boat as soon as they saw Adelman dart for the raft. Realizing that Adelman was too far away to reach, Hawk searched for an alternative. Nearby was a makeshift jet ski rental company manned by a guy sitting in a lawn chair who swiped listlessly at his phone.

Hawk handed his credit card to the man and dashed toward the water. Alex joined him, quickly settling onto one.

"What are you doing?" the man asked as he stood and scowled. "You have to sign a release waiver and some other paperwork."

"I'll do it when I get back," Hawk said as he hurriedly untied the rope from the dock cleat.

"That's not how this works."

Hawk ignored the man and backed up in the water. Alex was right behind him.

The attendant rushed over to make an effort to stop Hawk and Alex, but it was a feeble attempt. Yelling some threats toward them, the man threw his hands in the air as Hawk and Alex roared after Adelman.

Though he had a good head start, Hawk and Alex spotted him preparing to leave the harbor and get out into the open water. Hawk shifted in his seat as he assessed the situation and determined the best strategy for catching Adelman. With scores of nearby islands, Hawk's greatest fear was losing Adelman. Trying to find him on one of the islands after he vanished would be a daunting task—and likely a failure. Catching Adelman in the open water also proved challenging given the head start that he had. But Hawk was counting on his more nimble craft to navigate the ocean better than Adelman's raft.

Adelman remained about two hundred meters off shore, frequently checking over his shoulder to see where Hawk and Alex were. As they circled the island, a large cruise ship chugged into the harbor, blocking Adelman's path and creating a massive wake. Upon seeing his dilemma, Adelman veered away from shore, giving Hawk and Alex the angle they needed to catch him.

In less than a minute, Hawk roared up just behind the raft. Adelman drew his gun and started firing as he bounced along the choppy waters. Hawk and Alex ducked as the bullets flew harmlessly past. With the ocean liner's wake fast approaching, he decided to take it head on.

Adelman smashed into the wave and kept going but lost some of his speed. Hawk careened over the top, going airborne but managing to maintain momentum. Seconds later, Hawk pulled up next to the raft and dove inside. He landed hard but rolled over quickly to face Adelman. Using one hand to drive his watercraft, Adelman tried to steady his aim on Hawk. But Hawk darted to his left and then kicked Adelman's hand, knocking the gun over the side.

Adelman took his hand off the motor's throttle as the raft slowed down. Alex eased up next them and winked at Hawk.

"It's over," Hawk said.

"You can't take me back," Adelman said. "There's no extradition agreement here."

"I'm not here to take you back. We're here for the truth."

Adelman shook his head. "Trust me. You don't want to hear the truth about Obsidian."

"Try me."

CHAPTER 21

HAWK CINCHED THE ZIP TIE wrapped around Adelman's hands for emphasis. There was no way he was escaping, but Hawk couldn't resist the urge to yank on it once more. Adelman sat in the cabin of his catamaran at the table, what little hair he had left tousled during the windy ride back to his ship.

"You should probably start shaving that dome of yours," Hawk said as he sat down opposite of Adelman. "It'll help you look wiser."

Adelman sighed and shook his head. "You always were a little smart ass."

"Look, to be honest, I never thought I'd see you again after what happened on that last mission," Hawk said. "And as shocking as that day was, I still have a hard time believing you would ever betray your country like this."

Adelman set his jaw and stared out the window to his left. "You really don't know what you're getting yourself into. I've tried to warn you, but you're so damn stubborn."

"Being stubborn is a far better flaw than being a traitor."

Adelman pounded his fists on the desk. "I'm not a traitor, you moron."

"I'm curious how you're going to spin this because it's quite obvious that whatever you're doing, you don't have your country's best interests at heart."

"Hawk, you're never going to find anyone as patriotic as me, but you simply don't understand these people."

"By all means, please enlighten me."

Adelman sighed. "Where to begin?"

"How about at the beginning? We've got all the time in the world," Alex said.

"Actually, you don't. But I guess I'll get to that later if you want me to start at the top," Adelman said.

"Just get on with it," Hawk said.

"Well, Obsidian didn't just crop up overnight," Adelman said. "This is well-funded and well-organized group that has been planning this takeover for years."

"Takeover?" Hawk asked.

"It hasn't happened yet, but it will—and there's nothing you can do to stop it."

"We'll see about that."

"By the time I'm finished, you'll see just how futile any attempts are," Adelman said as he continued.

"This group has its tentacles in almost every single government on the planet and owns banks and media entities. Anything that can wield influence on the hapless public, you can bet Obsidian holds a stake in it."

"And what's their end game?" Alex asked.

"I wish I knew," Adelman said. "But I think it's safe to say that it would be pleased if it could force its will on the rest of the world."

"Why is that safe to say? What do you know that you're not telling us? Is there something they're planning?"

Adelman nodded. "Yeah, and it's going to significantly reduce the world's population, making Obsidian's goal of control much easier."

"So, what's it going to be?" Hawk asked. "Nuclear warheads, intercontinental ballistic missiles, dirty bombs?"

Adelman winced and then sighed. "No matter what you do, you can't resist these people. They have a way of forcing you to do their bidding. Resisting them is a mortal mistake."

"And you know this how?" Hawk asked.

"Unfortunately, I've seen others resist their initial overtures. The result was fatal. I'm a patriot, but I'm also not stupid."

"Perhaps, but you still haven't answered my

question," Hawk said as he narrowed his eyes. "What's being planned?"

"Obsidian is going to take over by deploying a virus of some sort. It's going to kill millions of people. Some of their estimates have casualties reaching as high as one billion people or more."

"That's insane," Alex said. "How could they possibly pull off something like that?"

"They have their ways."

"You mean they have people who have been coerced through nefarious means?"

"Blackmail, payoffs, you name it," Adelman said. "There's really nothing they won't do to get what they want. And it's far more effective than raising an army to battle against some of the most powerful forces in the world. Sabotage from within is their MO."

"And you were part of that strategy, weren't you?" Hawk asked.

Adelman looked down and closed his eyes as he shook his head. "This isn't who I ever wanted to be, especially when it came to doing something against my country. But we're not infallible. Maybe we need a change at the top as well as a transformation in the way we do things."

"And you think Obsidian could do that for us?" Alex asked.

Adelman shrugged. "It's possible. But I don't

really have a choice when it comes to my duties. If I don't do what they say, they'll kill me."

"This virus," Hawk said, "has it been released yet?"

"Not yet, but the day is drawing near. I don't know if they've announced their release date outside of the top level of leadership. They are very secretive. But it's only a matter of time before large portions of the western world's population are writhing in pain, wishing they had never been born."

"But you're sure they haven't released it yet?"

"Obsidian researchers are working on an antidote, though it hasn't been completed yet."

"Do you have any idea when it will be?" Hawk asked.

"Soon, very soon."

"I assume there's a lab somewhere handling all this," Alex said.

Adelman nodded.

She studied him closely. "So, where is this lab that's managing everything and developing an antidote?"

Adelman shrugged. "I have no idea. I was just called upon to make some introductions."

"Introductions to whom?"

"Important people who are most likely involved in all of this against their will."

Alex exhaled and looked skyward. "How do they contact you?"

Adelman nodded toward his left pocket. "There's a cell phone there that they gave me, which can be used anytime, day or night."

Alex pulled the chip out and copied all the information on the phone. She held it up and smiled. "You may not know all the answers, but this little thing right here is going to sing."

CHAPTER 22

Washington, D.C.

AFTER THE LONG FLIGHT back to Washington, Hawk and Alex barely had a day to recover before Blunt beckoned them back to the Phoenix Foundation offices to piece together all the new information. Hawk guzzled an energy drink just to wake up, while Alex loaded up on caffeine with a large drink from Starbucks. Blunt was already poring over some of the documents Alex had compiled during their trip home and sharing them with Black.

Wearing a big grin on his face, Blunt looked up at Hawk and Alex as they entered the conference room. "I always wanted to send you two on a trip to the South Pacific," Blunt said. "And from the looks of all these papers, I think it was a productive trip."

Hawk still wore his sunglasses and fell into a chair across the table from Blunt, while Alex took the adjacent seat.

"It's not exactly the kind of trip I'd hoped for, to be honest," Hawk said. "I wanted something a little more relaxing. Maybe read a Brad Thor novel on the beach and drink a few margaritas."

"That's not what it was like?" Black asked, a slight grin leaking across his face.

"This is all your fault," Alex said, pointing at Black. "You're the one who supposedly found Adelman. Then we had to go do all the dirty work."

"Well, you came back in one piece without any visible damage," Black said. "It must've not been that difficult for you."

"You don't know the half of it," Hawk said. "Let's just say Admiral Adelman wasn't exactly the most compliant target I've ever tracked down."

Blunt shrugged. "Regardless of what kind of challenges you had while you were down there, the results are outstanding. You were able to isolate all those calls from Adelman's phone and determine who was involved."

"Not exactly *who*," Alex said. "To me, it's more like a *what* was—and still is—involved."

"What kind of conclusions did you draw?" Blunt asked.

"This certainly isn't a simple investigation," Alex said. "There are plenty of moving parts, so you'll need to keep up. But the bottom line is I was able to use this phone number to search the dark web and discover linked accounts."

"And what did that tell you?" Blunt asked.

"It didn't tell me anything at first," Alex said. "These guys are good at covering their tracks, whether that's on the internet or through other means. But someone slipped up. That phone number was used to order large quantities of chemicals, the kind that you'd only need if you were dabbling in some sort of pharmaceutical endeavor."

She stood and walked around the table. "I'm sorry," she said. "That caffeine is really kicking in now."

Blunt chuckled and pointed at the papers in his hand. "In that case, please explain what's going on here."

"So I was able to map all the incoming calls to this phone," she said. "That provided a good visual for where this person was operating out of. I narrowed down all the potential sites that coincided with the cell towers nearby until I was able to draw more definitive conclusions."

"That Otto McWilliams was involved?" Blunt asked.

Alex nodded. "I'm not sure to what level, but on the very surface, it appears as though the former Pantheon Pharmaceuticals CEO is at least providing some sort of facility for Obsidian to work in. They have leases on a dozen buildings in a five-mile radius in Jacksonville, Florida."

"Very interesting," Black said. "You think McWilliams is part of the mastermind behind Obsidian?"

"Based on everything I've seen, it's hard to draw any final conclusions," Hawk said. "We must take into account the fact that McWilliams's office was where the request to hack the congressional network originated from, though Adelman was pretty adamant about the fact that Obsidian has a way of twisting everyone's arm until they yield to impossible demands. It's how the organization has chosen to operate, which seems to be pretty effective based on all the results up to this point."

"Whether McWilliams is willingly involved or not is inconsequential," Blunt said. "We need to find out what's really going on and what they're doing with all these chemicals."

"If they're creating an antidote as Adelman suggested, we can thwart their plans by uncovering the formula and open sourcing it to the world," Alex said.

"That's a great idea," Blunt said. "The only problem is we don't know where, if, or when that virus—or whatever it is—is going to be unleashed. And these aren't exactly the easiest chemicals to get your hands on. If a crisis begins to unfold, the demand will soar through the roof. Getting any antidote will be an arduous process at best, impossible at worst."

"That's why we need to stop this before it reaches that point," Black said.

"I know Senator Fontenot was insistent that his pal McWilliams couldn't be involved in any of this," Hawk said, "but the evidence says something different. I think he can be convinced to help us, especially if he understands what's at stake."

Blunt nodded. "I agree. Pay him a visit and see what Fontenot can do for us. We need to find out as soon as possible the exact location where Obsidian is developing this antidote before it's too late."

"I'm on it," Hawk said. "I'll get Fontenot to cooperate. He won't be able to say no once he sees all of this."

CHAPTER 23

SENATOR BERNARD FONTENOT stared wide-eyed at Hawk and Alex as they shared their hunches about Senator Otto McWilliams. With a broad range of initial reaction, Fontenot went from pacing around the room and shaking his head to sighing and collapsing onto the small couch in his office. He barely said a word but didn't have to.

"Are you going to be okay?" Alex asked.

Fontenot shrugged. "I guess it depends on what happens when I speak to Otto. If he admits to this—"

"He's not going to admit to this, and you know it," Alex said. "We want to discern if his level of involvement is something more serious, perhaps even voluntary."

Fontenot shook his head resolutely. "There's absolutely no way that Otto is involved in any of this on his own volition. They must have pictures of him cheating on Nancy or a wiretap of him taking some campaign money illegally. He would never betray his country like this."

"Maybe he doesn't view what he's doing as traitorous," Hawk said. "It's very possible that he's convinced himself that he is doing this because he loves his country, not because he hates it. And if he doesn't do something now, there is a possibility of even more danger in the future—a nefarious global organization running roughshod over our country and its freedoms."

"That's one theory," Alex said. "But we can't extrapolate the truth—or even some semblance thereof—if we don't question him about his involvement. We need to look into his eyes. *You* need to look into his eyes."

Fontenot hung his head for a moment before raising it. He set his jaw and eyed Hawk and Alex carefully. "Can I be sure that you two are going to make this as easy as possible for me?" Fontenot asked. "I really don't want to be put in an awkward situation with Otto. We've been friends for so long and—"

"We get it," Hawk said. "You're frat pals and have been through a lot together—and now you're both working as senators in a very cutthroat environment. To hear that one of your own betrayed you is a tough pill to swallow."

Alex nodded in agreement. "This isn't easy, but it's only going to get worse when reality strikes. When there's no more denying that he's not being strong-armed and cajoled into working for Obsidian, you'll feel differently. The sting of betrayal is not easily washed away—or forgotten. If what we believe about him matches up with what the team has been able to uncover, you would feel foolish for supporting him in the aftermath."

"Just promise me you won't throw him under the bus right away," Fontenot said. "I want to at least extend him that courtesy."

Hawk sighed yet nodded. "We can give him that, but we need to know the truth from you regarding Senator McWilliams. And by the truth, I mean everything that you learned or gleaned during your conversation with him, no matter how big or small. We need to find out what's truly going on."

Fontenot agreed, but Hawk wasn't confident that the Louisiana senator could deliver when push came to shove. However, there was no other viable alternative, not with an impending attack. Even without knowing what the date was, Alex concluded that the dissemination of the virus had to be near. The phone number affiliated with the Pantheon research labs had simply vanished from every website the researchers had ordered from, a systematic internet scrubbing.

"What we really need to know is if you're with us," Alex said. "Because if you're not, this operation is going to be doomed before it ever gets off the ground."

Fontenot stroked his chin but looked Hawk and Alex directly in the eyes. "I need to do this," Fontenot said, "partially for my own sanity but also for the sake of others. If I don't do anything, you'll be wondering all the time if there's a traitor walking the hallways of the Capitol building."

"And so will you," Alex said.

"I'll keep an open mind, but I just can't even fathom that being the case, even with all that damning evidence you brought me," Fontenot said. "There just has to be some other explanation."

"Why don't you find out firsthand tomorrow night at dinner?" Hawk said. "I heard he's a big fan of Le Diplomate."

* * *

FONTENOT SQUIRMED as Alex attached the wire to the inside of his blazer. Hawk straightened the senator's tie and then swept the lint off his shoulders.

"You look like a million bucks," Hawk said.

"What about presidential?" Fontenot asked.

"Hmm. I'm not sure that's quite the adjective I would use," Hawk said.

"With an answer as diplomatic as that, there's a future in politics for you, Hawk," Fontenot said with a chuckle. "I know the truth: I'm still a Cajun at heart.

There's nothing presidential about me, nor should I ever set my heart on reaching 1600 Pennsylvania Avenue other than to visit Noah Young."

Hawk shrugged. "You said it, not me."

"Would it hurt you two to at least pretend like I wasn't a fish out of water?"

Alex laughed. "No, but if you don't hold still, this wire is going to be as visible as the nose on your face. And that's the last thing you would want tonight."

She handed him a comb and told him to fix his hair one final time.

"This isn't a date," Fontenot said. "And I've been friends with Otto forever. If I look too put together, he's going to know something's up."

Alex reached up and tousled Fontenot's hair, wearing a smirk the entire time she was making his hair messy.

"Is this really necessary?" Fontenot asked again.

"Just finger comb it and then go up to the restaurant," Hawk said. "We'll be down here listening in on everything, so make sure you don't forget to ask him any of the questions we gave you on that list."

Fontenot tapped his temple with his right forefinger. "I've got a mind like a steel trap. So you don't need to worry. I'll remember them all. After all, it's how I got elected, being able to recall donors and constituents' names in a matter of nanoseconds."

"Okay, enough of you telling me about this memory of yours," Hawk said. "It's time for you to go out there and show me just how good it really is."

With a gentle nudge toward the door, Fontenot strode upstairs and prepared to enter Le Diplomate for his evening dinner date with McWilliams.

Le Diplomate was the hottest new eatery in the capital, drawing long lines of patrons hoping to get a bite of something with a little French flair. Based on its history and clientele, Le Diplomate was the place people went to demonstrate their vast array of French knowledge, particularly regarding the European country's cuisine.

Wednesday night at Le Diplomate meant Pork Milanese, a meal Fontenot considered scrumptious. His Cajun roots gave him a deep affinity for French food. His hankering for French dining rubbed off on McWilliams while they were are Harvard together. Years later, the two men continued to bond over such restaurant experiences.

Fontenot took a seat inside a small private room that couldn't hold more than a dozen people.

"When will the rest of your party be arriving?" asked the server tasked with covering the room.

"There will only be one more member of my party," Fontenot said. "And I can assure you that paying close attention to us in here will be worth your time," Fontenot said.

The waiter exited the room, closing the door behind him.

Seconds later, the door flung open again, but this time Otto McWilliams marched inside. With an ear-to-ear grin, he strode over to the table where Fontenot was. He stood, and the two men embraced.

"You're speaking my language," McWilliams said after they finished. "You know how much I love French food."

"Of course I do," Fontenot said. "I was the one who introduced you to it while we were at Harvard—or have you already forgotten?"

"Oh, I remember," McWilliams said. "There are some things I'll never forget, like how you turned down Melissa Butterfield after the game against Yale our junior year. For weeks afterward, I wondered what was wrong you."

"I didn't snub her—she just wasn't my speed."

"She was everyone's speed—fast."

"And loose," Fontenot said. "I don't care how beautiful a woman is, if she throws herself at men like Melissa did, I'm not interested. Nothing personal, but I can smell desperation coming a mile away."

"Yet you can't smell my desperation, can you?" McWilliams asked.

"What do you mean?" Fontenot asked. "What

are you so desperate about?"

McWilliams nodded. "I'm having to sell off my oil fields just to make ends meet. It's a rather difficult time."

"Well, I'm buying tonight," Fontenot said. "You order whatever you like. It's on me."

"That's very kind and generous of you, but that's not where I need cheering up. I've done something I shouldn't have."

"Go on," Fontenot said. "Get it off your chest."

McWilliams sighed. "I shouldn't be telling you this, but I feel like I must. That's part of the reason I'm somewhat depressed right now."

"What did you do?" Fontenot asked as he leaned forward in his seat.

"Look, I don't know, maybe I shouldn't burden you with this. I hate dumping my problems on top of other people."

"Even a good friend like me?" Fontenot asked.

"Fine. You'll probably laugh at me anyway," McWilliams said. "But the truth is I've been really depressed for quite some time about one of my business deals. I lost our house in the Caymans."

"It's not the end of the world. It happens. So, how did you lose this house? Bad business deal?"

"It wasn't in a deal," McWilliams said. "I gambled it away."

"Whoa."

McWilliams nodded. "Nancy doesn't even know about it yet. Please don't tell her. We've only got thirty days to get out or they're going to unceremoniously dump our things at the curb."

"You need to come up with something quickly."

"I haven't exhausted all my options yet, but time is running out. But that's not why you invited me here tonight, is it?"

Fontenot shook his head. "No, it's not. I brought you here to ask some very pointed questions."

"Questions about what?"

"About Obsidian?"

"Obsidian? What do you think I would know about them that you don't?" McWilliams asked. "We're on the same senate committee. You know what I know."

Fontenot stared intently at McWilliams. "Are you involved with them in any way?"

"Oh, come on, Bernard. You don't actually think I'd have anything to do with a group like that. I would never align myself with an organization like that in any way."

"Are you sure?"

"Seriously, is this what tonight was all about? Because if it was, I'm leaving right now. These accusations are absurd."

McWilliams stood and tossed his napkin onto his plate. He turned to walk away when a server entered the room. As McWilliams attempted to push his way past the man, he jammed a syringe into McWilliams's neck. A few seconds later, he tumbled to the ground.

Hawk, dressed in server attire, knelt next to McWilliams and checked his pulse before lugging him through a private exit and down to the restaurant's basement.

* * *

HAWK SLAPPED MCWILLIAMS several times in an effort to get him to wake up. The tranquilizer was only supposed to last about five minutes, but McWilliams was having a hard time regaining consciousness. Hawk rechecked the rope that bound the senator to the chair and then stepped back to watch and wait.

Behind Hawk, Fontenot paced around, muttering to himself before going after Alex and Hawk.

"This wasn't part of the deal," Fontenot said. "You never said anything about drugging him and interrogating him."

"Relax," Hawk said. "It's not like we're going to water board him or anything. We just need to get some straight answers out of him. And it was clear that wasn't going to happen from the way your conversation was going."

Fontenot scowled. "This was the plan all along, wasn't it? Use me as the bait to lure him here and then you question him."

"We couldn't just grab him off the street, could we?" Alex said. "We hoped it wouldn't come to this, but it's apparent that you're just too close—not to mention he thinks he can lie to you and get away with it."

"How do you know he was lying?" Fontenot asked.

"He's a politician and his lips were moving," Hawk said, trying to suppress a smile.

"I take offense at that. In case you haven't noticed, I'm a—"

"It was a joke," Hawk said. "Take it easy, will ya?"

Alex tried to dispel the growing tension. "We think it would be naïve at best, foolish at worst, to assume that the link between McWilliams and Pantheon and now Obsidian and Pantheon was just some weird coincidence. And from the sound of your conversation, you weren't ready to push back on him and discover the truth."

Before the conversation went any further, McWilliams started to stir.

Fontenot rushed over to him. "Hey, Otto, are you okay? It's me, Bernard."

McWilliams lunged toward Fontenot but was

stopped short due to the bindings.

"How could you do this to me?" McWilliams asked while glaring at Fontenot and struggling to get free.

"I—I didn't know this was going to happen," Fontenot said. "I was just supposed to ask you some questions, but then—"

"We need to talk," Hawk said.

"Who the hell are you?" McWilliams asked.

"I'm the man who's going to cut you loose if you tell me what I want to know."

"I'm not telling you a damn thing. Now get me out of here before I have you arrested for these shenanigans."

Hawk didn't budge. "I need you to tell us what you know about Obsidian and their plans to launch a devastating virus on the world."

"Maybe you didn't hear me the first time," McWilliams said with a snarl.

"Oh, I heard you," Hawk said. "I also heard you say this."

Hawk tapped a button on his phone, which played a snippet of McWilliams's conversation with Fontenot. After just a few seconds, Hawk stopped it.

"I'm sure Nancy would love to hear about your gambling problem and how you lost one of your homes because of your addiction," Hawk said. "Now, you'll answer what I ask or else your wife will find out all about this. Then we'll forward this to the ethics committee to review since you've been covering up your betting deficit with campaign donations."

McWilliams looked down and shook his head. "What do you want to know?"

"Why is Obsidian working out of some of Pantheon's labs?" Hawk asked.

"Convenience, I guess."

"You *guess*," Alex said, butting her way into the interview. "You know exactly why, so stop beating around the bush with us."

"Fine, I used some of my connections at Pantheon to help Obsidian get space in those labs. But I didn't really have a choice. They forced me to work with them."

"Forced you how?" Hawk asked.

"They told me they would show pictures from one of my previous affairs to my wife," McWilliams said.

Alex shook her head. "I'm not buying it. You're lying to us."

"I swear it's the truth," McWilliams said.

Alex snatched Hawk's phone and started tapping around on the screen.

"What are you doing?" McWilliams asked, the lines on his forehead creasing.

"I'm sending this file to your wife," she said.

"Okay, okay. Obsidian didn't threaten me like that. They told me they could guarantee me the chairman position on the senate intelligence committee if I assisted them in finding some lab space."

Fontenot walked deliberately toward McWilliams before raring back to punch him. Hawk grabbed Fontenot's forearm, stopping him just before he could make contact with McWilliams's face.

"You were responsible for blackmailing me," Fontenot said. "I thought we were good friends, fraternity brothers with a deep connection. And then you go and pull a stunt like this, something that could've ruined me—all so you could become chair of the committee? How could you do this to me?"

McWilliams stared at his shoes and remained silent.

"Now is not the time to clam up," Fontenot said, still being restrained by Hawk. "You start talking right now, or I'll tell Nancy myself about what you're doing."

McWilliams sighed, refusing to look Fontenot in the eyes. "I'm not proud of what I did. But I just—I don't know. I thought I should've been the one to chair the committee, and I saw an opportunity and I—"

"And you backstabbed one of your best friends in the senate," Fontenot said. "I never imagined you would turn out like this."

Hawk released Fontenot, who eased up and retreated to the far corner of the room.

"Obsidian is a dangerous organization," Hawk said. "We both know that. But we need to know where they're developing this antidote and when they plan on releasing this virus."

"I can tell you where they are," McWilliams said, "but I can't tell you anything about their plans. I just know it's going to happen very soon."

Hawk placed a piece of paper and pen on the desk in front of McWilliams before cutting him loose.

"Write down the address, and get outta here," Hawk said. "And don't think we won't be watching you."

CHAPTER 24

Jacksonville, Florida

AFTER A PLANNING SESSION during the short flight down to Jacksonville, Hawk awoke the next morning ready to uncover the scope of Obsidian's scheme as well as concoct a way to stop it. He was first in line at the Starbucks around the corner from their hotel, waiting to get Alex a latte. Though he wasn't sure how Black liked his coffee, Hawk figured the man's namesake might be a good bet.

When Hawk returned to the room, he was greeted by a gun pressed against his forehead.

"Is this how you treat everyone who brings you coffee?" Hawk asked.

Black holstered his weapon and took the cup offered to him. "This looks black."

Hawk nodded. "Is there a problem with that? I don't want to get shot for bringing you the wrong coffee next time."

240 | R.J. PATTERSON

"This is how I like it," Black said, his morning voice still gravely. "You did good, kid."

Hawk hated being called a kid, even though compared to most people in his field, he was. Titus Black only had five years on him at the most, but that was significant in the world of espionage. So much could happen during a short timeframe like that, things that could change a man forever—for better or for worse. Hawk wasn't sure if the scales in his life were even, but he intended to weigh them in his favor for good after stopping Obsidian.

Hawk placed Alex's drink on the nightstand and nudged her. "Time to get up, honey," Hawk said softly. "We have some monsters to catch."

She opened her eyes wide and then stretched, groaning as she grabbed the headboard behind her. "I can stay here and work in my pajamas while you two go out there and do the dirty work," she said. "I'm not in quite the same rush."

"True," Hawk said, "but you never know when you're going to have to come to our rescue. And if that time comes, do you really want to be wearing *that*?"

Alex shrugged. "Okay, I'll change. But then you two need to get going ASAP. Those fastidious researchers in the lab like to clear their minds and start their work before all the riff raff comes rolling in."

Hawk and Black suited up and took off outside. They linked up their com devices with Alex and made sure everything was in working order.

"You'll be happy to know I'm dressed in something far more appropriate for saving you two when the time comes," she announced.

Hawk threw his head back and sighed before shifting into gear and heading onto the interstate to reach the facility McWilliams had told them about.

"Do you have to save Hawk often?" Black asked with a sly grin.

After a sideways glance at Black, Hawk balled up his fist, shaking it playfully at his partner for the day's mission.

"It just depends," Alex said. "If he goes in guns blazing, he doesn't always have the best exit strategy."

"Good to know," Black said with a wink. "I'll make sure I don't let him race off without my consent or any discussion regarding an escape plan. I've found those are vital for survival."

"Should I recount all the times I've saved you, Hawk, or would you like to share them with your new partner?" Alex asked.

"Just finish setting everything up, Alex," Hawk said with a growl.

"Maybe you should've bought yourself a triple latte," Alex said. "You woke up feisty this morning.

Just make sure you channel all that aggression out on the numbskulls who want to infect the world with a virus."

"I'll let you know when we get there," Hawk said.

He turned off his coms and focused his attention on Black.

"It's not so bad to have someone watching your back, you know," Black said. "I'm sure she doesn't mind it when you get her out of a jam."

"I don't mind being saved, but it does remind me how fragile everything in our world is. I'm only one mistake away from either getting killed myself or worse—captured. Alex is always going to come after me, and one time she might not be able to rescue me. I'd have a hard time living with that."

Black punched Hawk in the shoulder. "You'll be fine, big man."

Hawk withdrew and eyed Black carefully. "I'm not sure we're there yet in our partnership."

"What do you mean?"

"You hitting me in the arm," Hawk said. "I barely know anything about you."

"You should know that Blunt trusts me, and that should be enough."

"But it's not for me. He's been fooled before."

"No one's doing any fooling here," Black said. "We're all on the same team, striving for the same goal."

"And what's that exactly?" Hawk asked.

"Eliminating Obsidian. It's a tall order, especially considering that Blunt had to join his number two team with me to make this happen."

Hawk smirked. "Number two team? You sure do think a lot of yourself."

"I've got a lengthy record of success—and I don't have anyone to save me. Instead, I have no margin for error. It's a scary way to operate in our world."

Hawk looked at his GPS and noticed that they were only five minutes away from the facility. He turned his coms back on. "We're almost there," Hawk said. "Be ready."

"I will," she said. "And I want you to know that was one of the sweetest things you've ever said about our relationship. I'd have a hard time without you, too."

Hawk furrowed his brow. "You heard all that."

"Yeah, Black didn't turn off his coms."

Black chuckled. "You really do need some coffee, Hawk."

"We'll talk later, Mr. Number One agent," Alex said. "We'll have to compare notes before I actually consider you to be a better assassin than Hawk."

"It'll be my pleasure," Black said.

Hawk exited the freeway and drove along a

surface street that ran parallel to the St. John's River. A few minutes later, he turned right into a nearly empty parking lot in front of a building that appeared all but deserted. A few cars sat near the entrance to the lab, the paint fading due to the searing Florida sun and unwavering humidity that settled over the area year round.

Hawk and Black got out and approached the front doors.

"Here we go," Hawk said over his coms.

The glass was papered up, preventing Hawk and Black from catching even a glimpse of what was inside. They shook the doors, but they remained locked. Despite raising quite a raucous, neither agent could attract the attention of anyone inside.

"Now what?" Black asked.

"Try the back entrance," Alex said. "There's a loading dock on the east side of the facility. And from what I can tell, it looks like there might be a way in there."

"Is the back door actually open?" Hawk asked.

"That's what it looks like," she said. "Go find out for yourself."

Both men hustled around to the back of the complex and raced up a ramp adjacent to the dock. A rollup door was raised with only opaque plastic strips hanging from the ceiling to prevent Hawk from seeing what was inside.

"This is unusual," Black said.

"Something's up, that's for sure," Hawk said.

Both men pushed their way inside the building and found a stark scene. Empty barrels of chemicals were stacked against the back wall on a pallet. Boxes of supplies were broken down and piled up at the foot of an industrial recycling bin. Against the far wall, a pair of haphazardly parked forklifts had pallets sitting on them. The floor was littered with paper, some of it shredded.

"Whoever was just here left in a hurry," Black said.

"There's nobody there?" Alex asked.

"Not in the warehouse," Hawk said. "And if you are working with chemicals, I can't imagine that you would just leave the back entrance to your lab open and unattended."

Hawk and Black wove their way through the maze of hallways and eventually found themselves near a corridor full of small labs. Broken vials were on the floor and desks in each room. Equipment was stripped out of the wall and tossed aside, treated as if it were trash.

The two agents worked their way down the dark passage, one room at a time. When they happened upon the last workroom, they found a man in a blue lab coat lying facedown on the floor. Hawk rushed over to the man and knelt beside him. He wasn't moving, his right hand still clutching a pair of glasses.

Hawk nudged the man gently before rolling him over. The employee groaned as he awoke. He rubbed his face with his hands and then blinked hard several times as he looked up at Hawk.

"Who are you?" the man asked. He had bruises all over his face and arms.

"We were about to ask you the same question," Hawk said.

"My name is Dr. Peterson."

Black crouched on his haunches and studied the doctor for a moment before speaking. "Who did this to you?"

Peterson swallowed hard and squinted as he looked up at Black. Then he closed his eyes and moaned, unable or unwilling to answer the question. Hawk wasn't sure which one it was.

"Dr. Peterson," Hawk said, gently shaking the man. "Dr. Peterson, who did this to you?"

Peterson rolled back over and opened his eyes. "Get far, far away," he said. "You don't want to be here when those men come back."

"What's there to come back for?" Black asked. "There isn't anything left in this place."

"But there is—and when they realize that they left something behind, they'll come get it."

"What did they leave?" Hawk asked.

Peterson turned his head slowly toward the corner of the room, gesturing toward it.

"They left something over there?" Black asked.

"You'll find it in those doors," Peterson said.

Hawk rushed over and flung open the doors to an industrial cooler. Wispy cold air rolled out, chilling him. He strode inside and found trays full of vials stacked against the far wall. Hawk grabbed one tray and brought it out with him.

"What's this, Doc?" Hawk asked.

"That's what they'll come back here to get," Peterson said. "That's the antidote."

"The antidote for what?" Black asked.

"For the virus that Obsidian is going to use to infect the world."

Hawk nodded. "And how do you know this?"

"Because I was here from the first day, though I never realized what we were really doing until it was too late. Then when I tried to get out, I was strong armed into remaining."

"Your family?" Black asked.

"My only daughter," Peterson said. "She's married now and has a child, but I don't think I could go on without her. I already lost my son and wife in a car accident about ten years ago. Losing my daughter would be too much to bear."

"But you resisted today?" Hawk said. "Why?"

"The more I thought about it, I decided to say the hell with it. If they killed my daughter, what difference would it make? She was probably going to die anyway if they launched this disease on the world."

"What's it called?" Black asked.

"They call it El Diablo, and they're ready to unleash it."

"Where did they go?" Hawk asked.

"Beats me," Peterson said. "All I know is that this place was cleaned out last night, and I heard one of the supervisors talking about Doom's Day."

"We would've all been screwed if you hadn't saved this antidote," Hawk said.

Peterson shook his head. "Nobody's saved yet. I need to reverse engineer this stuff—and I have no idea how much of the chemicals are available worldwide. Obsidian bought a ton of the ingredients, and they aren't cheap. You still need to stop it from launching, if you can."

Hawk stood and walked toward the door. "Alex, are you getting all this?"

"Unfortunately, yes."

"Call Blunt and tell him what Peterson has. We need to arrange to get Peterson to Washington and make sure that he has a lab with top security so he can start manufacturing this antidote when he gets there."

"I'll get that going, but I found something else of interest," she said.

"What is it?" Hawk asked.

"I started wondering about McWilliams," Alex said. "We should've never cut him loose."

"We couldn't hold a sitting senator like that, not without proof of him committing a crime."

"It's all a moot point now, but you said we would be watching him—and we weren't watching him closely enough."

Hawk sighed. "What did he do, Alex?"

"I tracked his private plane," she said. "He took off an hour ago from Jacksonville."

"Do you know where he was headed?"

"His plane is making an approach to land at the busiest airport in the world as we speak."

"Do you think that's where they're going to . . ."

"It seems like a logical choice to me," Alex said. "And given what we know, we can't afford to ignore this."

CHAPTER 25

Hartsfield-Jackson International Airport
Atlanta, Georgia

ALEX STUFFED ALL of the team's gear into a few bags and requested an Uber ride to the airport. With Obsidian already out of town with everything they needed to infect millions of people, she didn't have time to wait for the guys to swing back by and pick her up. They all needed to get in the air as soon as possible and hope that there was enough time to prevent the launch of a killer disease.

Instead of making polite conversation with the Uber driver, Alex slunk down in her seat in the back and called Blunt. The man driving didn't seem to mind as he tapped the steering wheel to the beat of the Bob Marley song blasting through his sound system.

"What did you find?" Blunt asked as answered his phone.

"It's not good," Alex said. "I haven't even had a chance to fully debrief with Hawk yet, but the

252 | R.J. PATTERSON

Pantheon lab was completely cleaned out."

Blunt let out a string of expletives, cursing so loudly that Alex had to hold the phone away from her ear while he ranted.

"You done?" Alex asked. "Because that's not even the worst of it."

"What could possibly be worse than that?"

"The disease is ready to weaponized since Obsidian now has an antidote for it," she said.

"And you know this how?"

"We found one doctor still alive after Obsidian gathered up everything and split," Alex said. "The poor doc had been beaten as well as threatened if he ever said anything. He somehow survived and managed to save a few hundred vials of the antidote."

"Can he help us?"

"He's volunteered to reverse engineer it so that Obsidian is unable to withhold the antidote from people who don't do their bidding."

"I'll get him anything he wants here in Washington."

"I figured you would," Alex said. "But there's more."

"Alex, I swear it's not a good idea for me to start popping antacid pills this early in the morning."

"Sorry, sir. I'm only reporting what I know."

"Go on."

"This is arguably the worst part—I tracked McWilliams's plane online. He was in Jacksonville last night, and they're making an approach to land at the Atlanta airport."

Blunt broke into another cursing fit. "What's that damn noise?"

"It's the Uber driver's music, sir," she said.

"A *what* driver?"

"Uber—oh, never mind. Look, can you help out? We need to call someone in Atlanta with Homeland Security and see if they can evacuate the airport before the whole place becomes Obsidian's private petri dish."

Blunt sighed. "I've got someone there I can call on, though I'd rather not."

"If you don't, millions of people could die and this disease could spread across the world in a matter of days—and it'd be too late by then."

"Damn it, Alex. You aren't making this any easier on me. If you only knew how much it pained me to call this asshole."

"Bite the bullet," she said. "This is for humanity. I'm sure you can justify trading a favor in this instance."

"Fine. I'll give him a call, but I want the record to show that I don't like this."

Alex chuckled. "Since when have you let the

record show that you liked anything?"

"I think the year was 1982. There was a nice chardonnay that came out of the south of France."

Alex rolled her eyes. "I'm at the airport. I've gotta run. We'll talk soon."

* * *

BLUNT HUNG UP with Alex and then buzzed Linda. He asked her to find the cell number for John Pembroke, the deputy secretary for Homeland Security. Pembroke had been a hotshot lawyer in Washington before running for congress in his home state of Minnesota. He only served one term before being trounced in his re-election campaign, but he served while Blunt was still in office. And the two clashed often over policy positions.

Despite their differences, Blunt maintained a semi-cordial relationship with Pembroke, which only boiled over when the Minnesota Vikings played the Dallas Cowboys. But Blunt knew the truth about Pembroke. While he was a friendly fellow, he had a dark side. Hawk chose to plug his ears and close his eyes whenever people started talking about what Pembroke was really into. Blunt didn't want to know. Plausible deniability was a politician's best friend, and Blunt intended to keep it that way. However, the thought of calling on Pembroke for a favor meant Blunt would have to dole out one in return. And that wasn't something he was excited about.

Blunt dialed Pembroke's number and waited for him to answer.

"As I live and breathe," Pembroke said after picking up. "If it isn't the great J.D. Blunt. I must be living right to get a call from you."

"Or not," Blunt said. "I could be calling to let you know that we're about to arrest you and throw you in prison—and that you better run."

Pembroke laughed. "Why on earth would you have to do such a thing? I live a quiet and clean life these days. As I recall, you're the one who should be on the run, hiding in the gray areas."

"I won't dispute that claim," Blunt said. "I've done many things to avoid other U.S. government operatives, but, no matter what I do, they always seem to find me."

"Those pesky FBI agents."

"Well, as you might have guessed based on the length between now and the last time I contacted you, I have a problem," Blunt said.

"Are you in trouble?"

"No, but thousands of innocent Americans might be in a matter of minutes if a terrorist group has its way at the Atlanta airport."

The mention of the Atlanta airport perked up Pembroke.

"What's going on?" he asked.

"There's a terrorist organization that has weaponized a disease and intends to disseminate it at the Atlanta airport this morning."

"That's insane," Pembroke said. "They're going to infect people flying all over the world."

"Yes, and then those people will infect their communities," Blunt said. "It's going to spread like wildfire, and there won't be much of a way to stop it."

"But you think we can by shutting down the Atlanta airport?" Pembroke asked.

"It's the only way. Of course if we do our jobs, it will look like nothing happened. But that's far more important than whether or not we look like we know what we're doing. Am I right?"

Pembroke was silent. All Blunt could hear was a long sigh and a few cars honking in the background.

"I know it's a lot to take in," Blunt continued, "but I' m telling you this so you can help thousands of people avoid getting infected and spreading a deadly disease all over the world. If there was another way, you bet I'd pursue it. But there isn't, so . . ."

"I understand," Pembroke said. "You want me to order a temporary shutdown of the Atlanta airport so we can sniff out any perpetrators?"

"You got it."

"Consider it done," Pembroke said. "Better not

make me look like a fool."

"I'd never do that in a million years, though you have chosen to be a fan of the Minnesota Vikings. That's being a fool to the nth degree. There's not much I can do for you there."

"We'll see soon enough," Pembroke said.

"So, you'll take care of that for me?" Blunt asked.

"As soon as I hang up, I'll give the order for the entire airport to be evacuated," Pembroke said.

* * *

HAWK, ALEX, AND BLACK landed at the Atlanta airport and raced over toward the commercial terminals. When they arrived, Homeland Security agents swarmed over the common areas. Bomb sniffing dogs moved up and down the different waiting zones, which had been cleared of all passengers.

Hawk found the agent in charge to learn more about what was going on.

"Tyler Goodman," the man said, offering his hand to Hawk.

"Pleased to meet you," Hawk said after introducing himself. "We're partially responsible for all of this."

"So you know who's behind this?" Goodman asked.

"I'm not at liberty to divulge all the details, but,

yes, I know who's driving this thing. What have you found so far?"

"A big fat nothing burger," Goodman said. "I don't even think I've heard any dog in this K-9 unit bark. I'm starting to think someone pranked you."

Hawk shook his head. "I doubt that. There are so many moving parts to this investigation that I'm not willing to rule it out, but all signs point to this being the place that if anything serious is going to happen, this is the ideal location where it would go down."

"And we're talking about a bomb, aren't we?" Goodman asked.

"No, your bomb dogs aren't gonna find a single thing that we're searching for."

"It'd be nice to know what that is now."

Hawk nodded. "We're looking for some device that can turn a liquid into mist. It doesn't have to be all that big—it just needs to be near a large number of people."

Goodman rubbed his temples with his fingertips. "I know I saw something in one of those locations earlier today."

"You think it was a device like I mentioned?"

"Maybe," Goodman said. "It was in the international concourse."

"That'd make the most sense," Hawk said.

Alex and Black struck off to search in other areas of the building, but Hawk sensed that he was onto something real.

Hawk and Goodman raced toward the trains and boarded quickly. In a matter of minutes, the airport transportation had taken them from one end of the facility all the way to the farthest reaches. Once the doors slid open, Hawk followed Goodman up a moving escalator until they reached the main lobby area.

Frantically searching all over the open space devoid of any people milling around, Goodman didn't find anything.

"Are you sure this threat is legit?" Goodman asked.

"It's real, all right," Hawk said. "We're just not entirely sure where it is."

"As in, you don't know if it's even at this airport?"

Hawk nodded. "Just keep looking."

After a few more minutes of searching, Goodman shook his head. "I think y'all were played as fools."

Hawk groaned and continued to scour the airport. Despite a thorough search, it appeared as if there wasn't any device capable of disseminating any disease into the air. Reconnecting with the rest of the team, Hawk discussed it over with Alex and Black. They didn't find a shred of evidence either.

Hawk volunteered to call Blunt and let him know the bad news.

"This couldn't get any worse," Blunt said. "Obsidian is running around with this disease just waiting to unleash it on the world and we don't have a clue where they are or where they're going to use it. Not to mention that I now owe John Pembroke a favor. Do you know how infuriating that is?"

"I'm sorry," Hawk said. "We were just following the evidence."

"No, you were chasing a red herring. Meanwhile, Obsidian has vanished from our radar."

Alex tugged on Hawk's arm as he continued his conversation. He held up his index finger and stared out the window in front of one of the gates.

"I think I know where they're going to strike," Alex whispered.

Hawk stopped. "Wait a minute," he told Blunt. "Alex has an idea of where they're going to strike."

"Where is it?" Hawk asked.

She pointed to the television screen where a story was airing about the final general assembly for the United Nations that was scheduled to take place tomorrow. President Young was slated to speak and offer closing remarks.

"What do you think about that idea?" Hawk asked.

"It certainly fits Obsidian's MO—infect the most powerful people in the country and only offer them the antidote in exchange for a favor," Blunt said.

"And use the ambassadors to infect every single nation on earth," Hawk said. "There's more of a guarantee to spread this disease worldwide using the UN as a launching point."

"Get back to Washington right now," Blunt said. "We need to figure out how we're going to stop this."

.

CHAPTER 26

Washington, D.C.

THE TEAM RECONVENED at the Phoenix Foundation offices at 2:00 p.m. to create a plan for handling a potential attack at the U.N. general assembly the following evening. Blunt announced that Dr. Peterson had arrived safely in Washington and had already been directed to the CIA's most technologically advanced lab. Even more encouraging was the fact that Peterson had already called him and told him that he had all the ingredients on hand to start mass producing the antidote.

"Do we even know how many shots of the antidote we'll need to administer?" Alex asked. "We're talking about potentially millions of people here."

"I told Peterson we wanted ten thousand to start with," Blunt said. "He's already ordered more, which should arrive within a couple days. But that should be enough to handle this event at the U.N."

"What else do we know about this disease Obsidian plans to spread?" Hawk asked.

Blunt gnawed on his cigar as he handed out prepared reports to all the team members. "Everything you want to know about El Diablo is in there. According to Dr. Peterson, it's actually a type of virus that presents very quickly but kills you slowly over the course of about two months. However, most doctors will believe it's something benign until it's too late. Victims' organs will start to shut down, and it's very painful."

"Sounds awful," Alex said.

"Yes, but the good news is that it's incredibly difficult to make," Blunt said. "You can only make it with this milk from this rare plant, some Latin name that I can't pronounce—but it's in that document somewhere. Anyway, they can only harvest the milk when it blooms, and that only happens once every seven years."

"Sounds like you're saying they don't have much of this El Diablo around," Black said, his head still buried in the report.

"That's exactly right," Blunt said. "Obsidian has one shot at this, according to Peterson."

"What are you thinking?" Hawk asked.

"I've thought about this a lot since I learned that information regarding the virus," Blunt began, "and I don't make this decision lightly. Typically, we would try to go after the virus and capture it, but not this time. I want Obsidian to disseminate it."

"What on earth for?" Alex asked, her eyes widening.

"If we make an attempt to snatch the virus and fail, we run the risk of this happening all over again."

"We won't fail," Hawk said.

Blunt grimaced. "While this team is the best of the best, you're not infallible. And I don't want to risk the possibility that this substance escapes the U.N. without being utilized. We'd be back to square one."

"But we'd have plenty of antidote to counteract the virus's effects," Alex argued.

Blunt nodded. "Perhaps, but the antidote needs to be administered within one week of contracting the virus. Otherwise, it's worthless. Even with all the antidote in the world, that would still leave plenty of people vulnerable to the effects of El Diablo."

"So, how exactly do you see this going down?" Hawk asked.

"According to Dr. Peterson, the virus needs to be ingested orally. It's odorless and tasteless, meaning they could place it in any drink served at the U.N. tomorrow night and no one would be the wiser."

"They're using a catering company," Black said.

Blunt pointed at Black. "You got it. I already had

a background check run on them, and two of the company's employees are former private security guards who served in Afghanistan and Iraq."

"That's pretty telling," Hawk said. "Looks like we don't have to wonder if this is where Obsidian is going to strike."

"No, Alex's hunch proved to be dead on, which is one thing that gives me confidence that we can thwart this attack."

Hawk shifted in his seat, lines creasing on his forehead. "I understand what you're wanting to do here, but I do have a big logistical question about all this."

"Shoot," Blunt said.

"If everyone at the U.N. gets infected tomorrow night, how do you expect the antidote to be administered? Do you think everyone is just going to sit around and wait for a nurse to roll up their sleeve and jam a needle into their arm?"

"As a matter of fact, I do," Blunt said.

"And how are you going to get people to do that?" Alex asked.

"I'm working on it," he said. "Now you three get to New York and get set up. We've got a busy thirty-six hours ahead of us."

CHAPTER 27

BLUNT WAITED PATIENTLY outside the door to the CIA's secret prison facility. Buried deep underground, the entry point was through what appeared to be the bottom floor of a parking garage. The prison was another fifty feet below it, accessible only through a narrow winding road. Blunt clasped his hands in front of him, anxious to get inside.

"Good to see you again, sir," the guard said as he flung open the gate. "Here for your weekly game of chess with Yuri?"

Blunt shook his head. He enjoyed sparring with the Russian spy who allegedly took his own life when he jumped from the Empire State building. But today, the visit was of a different nature.

"I need to speak with Talib Al-Asadi," Blunt said.

The guard shrugged. "That's different. Looking for a new way to construct a suicide vest?"

Blunt shrugged. "Maybe, maybe not."

"He is the expert, as you might already know."

"Why ask anyone else when the best expert in the world is in U.S. custody?" Blunt asked rhetorically. "That's what I say anyway."

The gate buzzed and slowly rolled open.

"Good luck in there," the guard said. "I hear Talib can be a real pain in the ass."

Talib Al-Asadi's incarceration came during a mission designed to stop a potential terrorist attack on the Golden Gate Bridge. He conspired with several other Al Hasib agents to blow it up during a celebration event that would've killed thousands of innocent Americans. Fortunately, Hawk stopped the potential bombing an apprehended Talib in the process. Instead of killing Talib on the spot, Hawk hoped that the prisoner might surrender some valuable information in captivity to help the U.S. thwart future incidents. But that hadn't exactly been the case.

For the past three years, Talib remained defiant, unwilling to offer up even a single shred of intelligence that could help the U.S. As a result, Blunt made sure that the CIA guards put the most pressure on Talib by refusing to grant him upgrades for anything. Food, free time, fun activities—it didn't matter to Talib. He wasn't willing to say anything to disparage his mates, even when collapse was all but imminent. But Blunt was certain that was about to change.

Two guards escorted Blunt down the long corridor of cell until they finally stopped at the next to last room on the right. One of the guards pressed the button on the side of his radio and asked his colleague in the control room to open the gate. A buzzing sound accompanied the latch springing open, granting access to the cell. The men strode inside and snatched Talib to his feet, forcing him back down the hall to a small interview room. After securing the prisoner to a chair, the guards exited, stopping briefly at the entryway to remind Blunt to signal them when he was finished.

"You are a foolish man," Talib said with a sneer. He barely glanced up at Blunt, staring off in the distance.

Blunt shrugged. "I've been called worse."

"I don't know what you hope I will say," Talib said.

"I don't want you to say much today. The word *yes* will be sufficient."

Talib grunted. "Depends on what the question is."

"It's a simple one," Blunt said. "Will you help me?"

A mocking grin spread across Talib's face. "Help you do what? Tie your shoes? Comb your hair? Shoot yourself in the head? I might help you with one of those."

"Perhaps I was wrong in assuming that you're the right person for this job," Blunt said before standing up and heading toward the door.

"You're always wrong in your assumptions about me."

Blunt nodded. "You're right. I thought you might be willing to listen to a proposal I have for you. But you're not apparently. And I guess you don't want to see pictures of your family either."

Talib's face fell, the snide glare exchanged for a wide-eyed longing. "Maybe we can have a conversation."

"I don't need a conversation—I need an answer," Blunt said. "I have a few photos, even a short video. I'll let you watch the images for thirty seconds, and then we will have a very serious talk. Understand?"

Talib nodded.

Blunt strode back across to the table and then sat down on the opposite side of Talib. Swiping on the phone's screen, Blunt called up the slideshow and held it out so Talib could see it. Photos of his family faded in and out. He smiled as he watched one of his son, laughing at what appeared to be a birthday party. But the smile quickly faded as a video captured his family more recently.

"What is this?" Talib demanded as images of his children wearing tattered clothes and dour looks replaced the happier times. An image of his wife appeared where she looked dirty and tired.

"What does it look like to you?" Blunt asked.

"That's not possible," Talib said. "They look . . ."

"Poor?" Blunt asked, finishing Talib's thought.

"But they can't be. Al Hasib promised to take care of them."

"I'm sure he did," Blunt said. "But Karif Fazil doesn't always follow through on his promises, does he?"

Talib glared at Blunt. "Don't try to fool me. I know he's dead."

"Maybe he is, maybe he isn't. But that's irrelevant to our conversation. Karif Fazil failed to deliver on the one promise he made to you—that he would take care of your wife and children if anything ever happened to you. Instead, your family struggles to live in poverty."

"Why are you showing me this?" Talib asked.

"Because I can change all this if you're willing to help me."

Talib threw his head back and exhaled slowly.

"I know this is a tough decision for you," Blunt said, "but it doesn't have to be. We can take care of your family, give them a new start with a new home."

"In the United States?" Talib asked.

"It doesn't have to be, if you would prefer otherwise. We can relocate them wherever you like with more than enough money for your children to grow with everything they'll ever need."

"If I help you, am I going to die?"

Blunt shrugged. "I'm not sure. It depends on how things go. However, I will tell you that I'm a man of my word. Despite your misguided principles, your family doesn't deserve to live in squalor. I will make sure that your sons grow up knowing what a good man their father was."

"And what if I don't?"

"Your children may die anyway in the most devastating terrorist attack this world has ever seen," Blunt said.

"And you need my help to stop it?"

Blunt nodded. "What do you say? For your family?"

Talib sighed and looked down. "I will help you, but may the wrath of Allah fall upon you if you don't keep your promise."

"We might have different ideas about what this world should be like, but I swear on my mother's grave that I will personally ensure your family has everything they need."

"Then I guess we are now partners," Talib said.

Blunt signaled for the guards and hoped that Talib wouldn't renege on his word.

CHAPTER 28

United Nations
New York, New York

THE NEXT AFTERNOON, the U.N. General Assembly hall filled up to capacity a half hour before United States President Noah Young was scheduled to speak. Hawk sensed the palpable energy in the room, which buzzed with anticipation. While the U.N. held its meetings in New York, several years had passed since the sitting U.S. president had addressed the ambassadors. And given all the unrest in the world, everyone wanted to hear from Young.

The atmosphere was electric and festive in the final session before summer break. While some ambassadors wouldn't return in the fall as their countries would appoint new representatives to take their places, others anticipated an important message to take back to their leaders about the direction of the world. Regardless of how everyone felt about the role of the United States within the U.N., anything the president said carried tremendous weight. And this time was no different.

Hawk, Alex, and Black had a vigorous debate with Blunt about whether or not they should alert President Young to the impending danger. They all concluded that it wouldn't be the best move. While Young could keep a secret, he wore his emotions on his sleeve. Blunt was certain that Young would act suspicious one way or another. And what he needed to convey in the meeting was strength.

The Phoenix Foundation's three agents entered the general assembly under the guise of security. Blunt finagled uniforms and security posts for all three of them after having a frank conversation with the head of U.N. security about a potential threat and urging him to let the team take charge should anything happen.

Alex initially hung back in the security room, watching monitors and observing movements in the lobby and the floor of the main hall. Hawk and Black patrolled the lobby, searching for the suspicious catering company serving the ambassadors. Neither task was all that exciting, but the main purpose was to watch out for a potential change in the way the caterers were serving people. Every drink had the potential to carry the virus—and Hawk and company decided to act as if that was the case.

A bell sounded, signaling for everyone to head to the main hall to hear the next speaker. Most everyone complied, much to Hawk's relief. The last thing he wanted to do was make a scene with some representative who was vying to sneak out early.

When President Young took the podium, he appeared confident and in command from Hawk's perspective. As many times as Hawk had seen Young speak over the years, it was one of the best speeches he had ever given.

"In the face of our changing world, now is not the time to shrink away from all the many challenges facing us," Young said. "Instead, it is time to stand up and face them all head on. We must be bold and courageous, staring down the terrorists who would prefer that we cower at their mere presence. If we want to create a world that's inviting to all with equal opportunities abounding, we can't abdicate our positions or yield them for a comfortable lifestyle. This is the time we make a stand for what we believe is right in this world, not kneel before the thugs who would prefer to keep us hiding in fear."

The assembly rose to its feet, giving Young a rousing applause. Hawk knew the message meant different things to different people, but it ultimately served as a clarion call to work together. The plea for unity was evident to even the casual bystander, though

Hawk wondered how many would heed it.

Once the meeting was convened, everyone began to mill around in the lobby for hors d'ouevres and drinks. A string quartet played classical pieces in one corner of the room while ambassadors chatted with each other. By the time most people had filtered out of the main hall, Hawk heard the message on his coms.

Hawk hustled over to President Young's team, which was slowly working its way through the crowd toward a back exit.

"Mr. President," Hawk said, getting Young's attention.

"What are you doing here?" Young asked as he furrowed his brow.

"There's a threat—and I need you to trust me right now," Hawk said. "Down the hall on the right, there's a room set up to administer an antidote to you and everyone with you. It's a must that everyone complies or else they could die."

"What are you talking about?" Young said. "I wasn't informed of any threat by my security detail."

"I know," Hawk said. "We'll explain later, but it's imperative that you comply or else everyone could die and thousands more will be infected."

Young sighed. "We're going to have a long talk about this later."

"Absolutely, sir," Hawk said. "Now if you'll please come with me."

Hawk led Young, his aides, and the Secret Service agents to the small room set up where a group of doctors and nurses waited. Once the last person received a shot, they were dismissed but told that another team waiting at Air Force One would be there make sure that they were no longer an endangerment to the public.

"Young and company are clear," Hawk said into his coms.

"Then it's time," Blunt said.

Hawk and Black secured all the doors leading to the outside, except for one. While it remained unlocked, Hawk stood next to it, awaiting the arrival of one person in particular.

"The doors are secured," Hawk said. "Alex, it's time for you to join us."

"Roger that," she said.

"Looks like everything is ready," Blunt said. "So I'm sending him in."

Blunt had barely finished getting the words out of his mouth when the fire alarm sounded.

"What's going on?" Blunt asked.

"Someone pulled the fire alarm," Hawk said.

"It's a hoax," Blunt said. "They're trying to scatter everyone. Do whatever you need to do to keep everyone inside. He's on his way."

Hawk stepped forward and raised his hands. "Please remain calm. There's nothing to worry about. It's just a malfunction. There's no fire."

He was so focused on easing the tension in the room that he didn't see the door open behind him.

"That's right," a man roared above the ringing. "Don't any of you go anywhere."

Hawk spun around to see a Middle Eastern man holding open his coat to display the bomb strapped to him.

The man hustled up onto the steps so that he could be heard more clearly. "If anyone leaves, I'm going to detonate this bomb."

CHAPTER 29

HAWK WATCHED TALIB AL-SADI hold his hands up in a gesture of surrender as several U.N. guards surrounded him, guns trained on his chest. Talib clutched a small device in his right hand. He had yet to explain what it was, but everyone there understood it to be a dead man's switch. If he was shot and his finger fell off the button, the bomb would detonate.

Two U.N. security personnel moved in on Talib as the ringing from the alarm finally stopped.

"That's far enough," Talib said as he stared down the duo and shook his hand containing the small object.

Hawk moved stealthily behind the crowd before hustling up a back stairwell to ease into position atop the bannister. He glanced at Alex, who was still guarding one of the doors. She nodded at him, giving him the signal that she was ready. Closing one eye, Hawk used his scope to hone in on Talib's neck. He waited patiently for Talib to stop shifting his weight from one foot to the other.

"Blunt, what did you tell this guy?" Hawk asked over the coms. "He's so nervous he looks like he might throw up."

"I told him he could die, though I didn't tell him that you'd be the one taking him out. Talib would have seriously tried to kill you if he knew the man who prevented him from getting all his virgins in the afterlife was in the same room tonight."

"He'll get over it," Hawk said.

Talib stopped moving just long enough for Hawk to decide to fire. He steadied his hand one final time before squeezing the trigger. The shot hit the intended target in the exact spot Hawk had aimed for. Talib grabbed his neck before toppling to the ground.

A gasp emanated from the onlookers, almost as if they were waiting for the bomb to detonate and everyone to be dead. But the device was still in Talib's hand. A pair of ambassadors edged toward Talib's body, ready to hold down the switch. But before the men got too close, Talib's hand fell open and the switch rolled off the end of his fingers and onto the floor.

Another collective gasp, this time louder than before.

"We're all gonna die," one ambassador said as he

collapsed and covered his head with his hands, as if he was awaiting that fatal moment.

Others joined him—but nothing happened. The small device clinked on the marble surface and rolled a few feet. Hawk raced down the steps toward Talib's body. Kneeling down to check Talib's vitals, Hawk nodded at Alex, who immediately stepped up and started explaining the situation, while Hawk grabbed Talib and dragged him to one of the nearby administrative offices.

"The package is secure," Hawk said into his coms.

"Ladies and gentlemen, I need you all to remain very calm," Alex said. "I'm sure you have plenty of questions, but the most important thing you need to know is this: you've all likely contracted a deadly virus through any of the drinks that you consumed here today. We've been following a terrorist organization for quite a while now, and we discovered only hours prior to this event that there was a plan in place to infect everyone here. It was the best way to transmit this awful virus all over the world without anyone realizing it until it was too late. However, you cannot leave until you've received a shot with the antidote and have a wristband attached. You will then be tested one hour later to make sure you aren't a threat to spread the virus."

"How do we know you're telling the truth?" one of the Russian ambassadors asked, shaking his fist. "How do we know this is not some ploy by the Americans?"

Other ambassadors joined in, nodding vigorously.

"You'll just have to trust us," Alex said. "But you're not getting through those doors without a shot."

The ambassador started to charge toward the only open door. Hawk fired a tranquilizer dart into the man's back. He took two more steps before he collapsed.

"Anyone else?" Alex asked. "Okay, good. Now let's all return to the main hall where we will process you."

A team of doctors and nurses contracted by the Phoenix Foundation poured into the room and set up a handful of stations in every corner to begin administering the shots. Above each post was a sign that delineated where each country's representatives were to go. Hawk and Black patrolled the area, making sure everything remained calm.

"Are all the doors locked?" Blunt asked over the coms.

"They are now," Black said. "I double checked them myself."

"We have to be certain," Blunt said. "If one person gets out, it could spell disaster."

"How are things looking on the outside?" Hawk asked.

"As of right now, it's quiet," Blunt said. "Not a soul moving near the doors. But you need to keep an eye out for anyone who looks shady. Someone from Obsidian might still be inside."

"I couldn't find a single person with a catering uniform on," Black said. "It's like they vanished."

"They're still here," Alex said, joining the conversation. "I just found one of their outfits in a trashcan in the ladies room."

"The medical staff has a manifest of everyone who is supposed to be there," Blunt said. "We should be able to identify the perpetrators after every authorized person there has received their shots."

Hawk milled around the main hall for a few minutes to observe the situation. While many ambassadors still wore worried looks on their faces and spoke in hushed tones, everyone remained calm.

"Everything looks good in here," Black said.

Hawk nodded. "I'm going to sweep the perimeter."

While Blunt had been monitoring the outside, he hadn't reported anything out of the ordinary since sending Talib in to keep the assembly from fleeing.

But that quickly changed.

"Hawk," Blunt said, "we've got a problem. Someone just exited one of the side doors and is heading across the street. And he's not wearing a wristband."

CHAPTER 30

HAWK BROKE INTO a sprint as he raced in the direction Blunt guided him. The scene across the street was a busy one with plenty of pedestrians clogging the sidewalk on a warm New York evening.

"You need to describe this guy to me so I know who I'm looking for," Hawk said.

"He's wearing a suit but no tie," Blunt said. "He looks like he's of Middle Eastern descent and balding."

"So, an old guy?"

"Maybe. It's hard to tell from the grainy footage I have. He has a goatee that appears to be gray."

"That's helpful," Hawk said. "But I'm still not seeing him."

"He just crossed the street and is heading east on Forty-Third."

Hawk darted through the intersection, stopping a few times to avoid getting hit by oncoming cars. Once he reached the other side, he hustled along the sidewalk as he searched for the escapee.

"If this guy is infected, could he already be infecting others?" Hawk asked.

"Not yet, according to Dr. Peterson."

"Well, that's about the only thing we have going for us here."

Hawk continued scanning the area in front of him.

"Do you see him yet?" Blunt asked.

"Not yet."

"I think he just went into the coffee shop on the corner."

Hawk bulled his way through throngs of people walking in the opposite direction, staying light on his feet. Once he went inside, Hawk spotted a man talking on his cell phone that fit the description Blunt had given.

"You see him yet?" Blunt asked.

"I think I've got him," Hawk said.

He rushed across the room toward the man, who cast a sideways glance toward Hawk. As he neared the table, the ambassador shoved it over in Hawk's direction before dashing out a side door. Hawk scrambled to regain his footing before hurdling over a few chairs and following the man outside.

When Hawk reached the curb, he watched as the man climbed into an SUV with diplomatic plates.

Searching for a way to continue pursuit, Hawk saw a motorcycle with the owner taking off her helmet. Hawk handed her his cell phone and wallet.

"I need to borrow your bike," Hawk said. "I'll bring it right back."

"What?" she said. "No."

Hawk was undeterred by her response and grabbed the keys from her hand and boarded the bike.

"Sorry," he called back as he turned the key and then kick started the engine. "I wouldn't do this if weren't important. Stay right here."

Hawk eased off the brake and onto the accelerator. Once he had a feel for how the bike handled, he took off after the SUV, which was turning up ahead at the next intersection.

"We've got a live one," Hawk said. "I'm on a motorcycle now, and that ambassador is in a black SUV."

"I see you," Blunt said. "The car is turning right."

"Roger that."

Hawk sped up and was only a few spots behind when the light turned yellow. Predictably, the SUV jammed on the gas and raced ahead. While Hawk could still see the car, he knew he was running out of time. He eased into the space between the lanes and revved the engine before speeding forward. Swerving to avoid a van in the cross street, Hawk maneuvered in and out of several cars, performing a meandering U-turn until he worked his way back across the intersection. The SUV had almost vanished from view by the time Hawk returned to a straight route, but he watched the ambassador turn left.

"You're losing him," Blunt said. "He just turned left onto Forty-Seventh Street. Stay with him."

"I can still see him," Hawk said.

He blew through two intersections and nearly lost control as he rounded the corner in pursuit. The slower traffic enabled him to make up some ground as he edged nearer than he'd ever been.

Once the flow of traffic picked up again, Hawk zoomed up next to the ambassador and motioned for him to pull over. He couldn't see inside the tinted windows, but he didn't have to in order to know what the driver was thinking.

A sharp jerk to the left sent the SUV careening into Hawk's lane. He eased on the brake and let the car whip by. Hawk gathered himself and made another approach. This time, the driver stomped on the brakes.

Hawk veered left, just missing a collision.

Moments later, they approached another intersection. This time, the driver jerked the steering wheel even harder to the left, clipping Hawk and sending the car into a spin. Vehicles traveling in both directions came to a screeching halt. Hawk tried to maintain his balance but lost it and skidded along the ground before coming to a stop near the curb. He remained still for a moment, unsure if he'd broken any bones. Based on the way he felt, he was almost certain that he had.

"Are you still alive?" Blunt asked.

"He can't get rid of me that easily," Hawk said with a slight chuckle that turned into a cough. He slipped his hands into his pocket and made a move to get up when a foot stomped on his chest.

Opening his eyes, Hawk looked up to see the ambassador.

"I will not allow you Americans to pump me full of your poison," the man said.

Hawk spotted a couple of men who appeared to be guards flanking the ambassador. With a slight nod, Hawk turned to the side and spit out some blood.

When the man spun around in the opposite direction, Hawk grabbed the man's leg and jammed a syringe into his calf. He screamed as he fell to the ground.

"This man is trying to poison me," the ambassador said.

Hawk shook his head. "No, I just saved your life."

Pedestrians stopped to take in the scene, many

of them filming the interaction with their cameras.

Hawk looked down as he staggered to his feet. He climbed onto the motorcycle, wincing in pain. Gritting his teeth, Hawk kick started the bike to life and slowly drove away from the scene.

"Nice work," Blunt said.

"I want a raise," Hawk snapped before turning off his coms.

Hawk returned the bike to the owner, who was still standing on the corner where he left her. She was speaking with a pair of police officers, recording her account of the brazen theft as she held up the phone and wallet to the cops. Hawk snatched them out of her hand and then dug into his wallet and handed her a card.

"I had a little accident," Hawk said. "Call the number on the back of that card tomorrow morning and tell them what happened. We'll make everything more than worth your time."

One of the cops grabbed Hawk by the arm. "You were the punk who stole this pretty little lady's bike?"

"I borrowed it," Hawk said.

The officer set his jaw and glared at Hawk. "Borrowed it? You think you can just commandeer someone's bike for a little joy ride and there won't be any consequences?"

Hawk looked at the woman. "Do you want to press charges now?"

She scowled as she looked at him and then back down at the card.

"Come on, lady," the other officer said. "We don't have all day."

"I guess not," she said. "He looks like a trustworthy fellow."

One of the cops laughed. "Do I need to remind you that this is New York City?"

She looked Hawk up and down. "I'm taking a flier on this one."

"Good call," Hawk said before he spun and walked away.

Hawk turned his coms back on and limped along the sidewalk toward the U.N. building.

"How's everyone doing?" Hawk asked.

"We just completed testing," Alex said. "Everyone appears to be showing no ill-effects of the virus. We're going to begin releasing everyone now."

"Hold popping the champagne corks," Blunt said. "I'm getting a call now from the head of U.N. security."

Hawk waited for Blunt to report back after hearing him say goodbye.

"Good news?" Hawk asked.

"That ambassador you chased down, Hawk,

wasn't the only person to break out," Blunt said.

"There was another one?" Black asked.

"Yeah, but nobody knows who he is."

CHAPTER 31

HAWK AND ALEX joined Black and Blunt at the Phoenix Foundation offices the next morning. The short flight from New York to Washington resulted in a poor night of sleep, but the team was summoned together per order of President Young.

Hawk eased into his chair in the conference room, holding an ice pack on his ribs.

"That was quite a tumble you took last night," Blunt said. "I thought for sure you broke something."

"A rib, maybe two," Hawk said. "I'll find out this afternoon when I go to the doctor. But that doesn't matter now, does it? We stopped Obsidian from taking the whole world hostage."

"For now, anyway," Black said. "We still need to find out who's really in leadership here and start rooting them out."

"No rest for the weary," Alex said, nursing her

cup of coffee.

Linda buzzed in over the phone's intercom system to let the team know that President Young was now on the line. She patched him in.

"J.D., I just wanted to tell you how grateful I am that you were able to eliminate that threat last night at the U.N.," Young said.

"Just doing our job," Blunt said.

"Next time, how about you give me a heads up, even if you are worried about a potential leak?"

"Sorry, Mr. President," Blunt said. "It's not that we didn't trust you. But we needed to keep the loop tight to avoid missing our opportunity to squash El Diablo. Unfortunately, we still don't know much about this group's leadership. We just know how they play—and they're making an unprecedented power play."

"I heard one of the ambassadors escaped without receiving the antidote," Young said.

"Hawk tracked him down and administered it on the street."

"Damn fine job, Hawk."

"Thank you, sir," Hawk said.

"Well, thank you to all of you, and keep up the good work." Young hung up, and the room fell silent.

"He doesn't know, does he?" Black asked.

Blunt shook his head. "We decided not to tell him about the mystery man who snuck out."

"Why not?" she asked.

"We don't need to trouble the president with things like that. It wasn't anyone who was there in an official capacity, so it was likely one of the terrorists responsible."

Alex leaned forward in her chair, her elbows resting on the table. "Nice deduction."

Blunt eyed her closely. "Do you know something else about the escapee?"

"I know he's not quite the mystery man today that he was last night."

"What do you mean?" Blunt asked.

"Last night, I entered the screenshot from the U.N. security feed into the CIA's database. We couldn't find anything on him, but we did find another picture he was in."

"We have his picture on file?" Black asked, "But we don't know who he is?"

"Just a cameo of sorts, captured with another person we know all too well," Alex said.

"Who?" Blunt asked.

"I found a shot of our mystery man with none other than Evana Bahar, Al Hasib's new leader," she said.

"I'm sure she'll be excited about helping us," Hawk said.

"That is if we can find her," Alex said. "She's

become a virtual ghost since last we saw her last in Cuba."

"Planning something big, no doubt," Black said.

Blunt clipped the end of a cigar he pulled out of his coat pocket. He jammed the stogie into his mouth and bit down hard. "That's another mission for another time," Blunt said. "There will always be some other evil to vanquish, but we need to celebrate this win today."

"Roger that," Alex said.

"Oh, one more thing," Blunt said as he reached underneath the table and flipped a switch. The monitor on the wall came alive, and a dark image started to populate the screen.

"What's that?" Hawk asked as he strained to make out the image.

"That is Otto McWilliams," Blunt said. "The CIA caught him last night. He's not going anywhere for a long time."

The team dished out compliments to one another about the mission for the next ten minutes before dismissing. Everyone stood and started to file out of the room.

"Hawk, if you've got a minute, I want to speak with you," Blunt said.

Hawk nodded and stopped as everyone else cleared out. He walked back over toward Blunt, who hadn't moved from his seat at the head of the table.

"What is it, boss?" Hawk asked.

Lines creased Blunt's forehead as he swallowed hard before answering. "I didn't want to tell you this in front of everyone and ruin the celebratory moment that we all needed, but there's something you need to know."

"What's wrong?"

"It's your mother," Blunt said. "They found her this morning dead on her front porch."

"What? How?"

"I could scarcely believe it myself when I first heard," Blunt said. "You know how much of a saint I thought she was."

Hawk still stared slack-jawed. "I thought nobody knew where she lived."

"Apparently, someone found out and stabbed her to death in her bed and then dragged her body onto the front steps. Then the killer left a message in her blood on the front porch."

Tears streamed down Hawk's face as he slumped into a chair and sobbed quietly. After a couple of minutes, he composed himself and stood up. He felt his face flush red with rage.

Setting his jaw and narrowing his eyes, Hawk stared with a steely gaze at Blunt. "What was the message?"

"The note was: 'Tell Brady he's next.'"

"Bastards," Hawk said. "Someone's gonna pay."

"They sure are," Blunt said. "They sure are."

THE END

ACKNOWLEDGMENTS

I am grateful to so many people who have helped with the creation of this project and the entire Brady Hawk series.

Krystal Wade was a big help in editing this book as always.

I would also like to thank my advance reader team for all their input in improving this book along with all the other readers who have enthusiastically embraced the story of Brady Hawk. Stay tuned ... there's more Brady Hawk coming soon.

ABOUT THE AUTHOR

R.J. PATTERSON is an award-winning writer living in southeastern Idaho. He first began his illustrious writing career as a sports journalist, recording his exploits on the soccer fields in England as a young boy. Then when his father told him that people would pay him to watch sports if he would write about what he saw, he went all in. He landed his first writing job at age 15 as a sports writer for a daily newspaper in Orangeburg, S.C. He later attended earned a degree in newspaper journalism from the University of Georgia, where he took a job covering high school sports for the award-winning *Athens Banner-Herald* and *Daily News*.

He later became the sports editor of *The Valdosta Daily Times* before working in the magazine world as an editor and freelance journalist. He has won numerous writing awards, including a national award for his investigative reporting on a sordid tale surrounding an NCAA investigation over the University of Georgia football program.

R.J. enjoys the great outdoors of the Northwest while living there with his wife and four children. He still follows sports closely. He also loves connecting with readers and would love to hear from you. To stay updated about future projects, connect with him over Facebook or on the interwebs at www.RJPbooks.com and sign up for his newsletter to get deals and updates.

Printed in Great Britain
by Amazon